'I want you to marry me.' Luke was watching her intently but Celina couldn't decipher the expression in his eyes.

As in the coffee-shop, she heard herself exclaim, 'You're mad! Besides, we've been over that already. I don't know what your game is, but you can definitely count me out.'

'You're wrong, Celina. I've never been more serious in my life. Why don't you let me explain?'

'What's there to explain? You've never liked me, never considered me good enough for Danny, and, if I'm not good enough for him, how could I possibly measure up to standard for his fastidious brother? No, you're laughing at me, dangling a carrot for some devious motive of your own.'

Luke replaced the cup on the table and leaned forwards, the lines of his body tense and urgent. 'I'm not asking for a conventional marriage. No, Celina, I want a marriage of convenience. I want a woman with more than a grain of sense who'll allow me the freedom to go my own way, live my own life. I want a woman who'll look good at my side when I'm entertaining, and, more importantly, who will understand when Miss Right comes along, and will step aside without any fuss and fade away into the background. I want *you*.'

SUBSTITUTE HUSBAND

BY

MARGARET CALLAGHAN

MILLS & BOON LIMITED
ETON HOUSE   18-24 PARADISE ROAD
RICHMOND   SURREY   TW9 1SR

*First published in Great Britain 1991
by Mills & Boon Limited*

© Margaret Callaghan 1991

*Australian copyright 1991
Philippine copyright 1992
This edition 1992*

ISBN 0 263 77401 5

*Set in Times Roman 10 on 11 pt.
01-9201-59429 C*

Made and printed in Great Britain

CHAPTER ONE

'HE ISN'T coming,' sneered the familiar voice at her elbow. 'Why don't you face the facts, Celina? He's stood you up. He isn't going to show now, and surely you must know it? You might just as well go home.'

Celina stared hard at the wall in front of her, trying not to listen to the words. She bit her lip, tasting blood, the sudden stinging sensation triggering her tears. Impatiently she blinked them away. She wouldn't cry. Not here. Not yet. Besides, it was only her pride that was dented. Just her stupid pride. She could always salvage that, couldn't she, for the next half-hour at least? After that, well, it really wouldn't matter. If only *he* would go away and leave her alone.

'He isn't coming,' she heard repeated mildly, just the merest hint of triumph in the tone. 'Danny's changed his mind. You can wait all day if you want to, but you're wasting your time.'

She spun round, facing him for the first time, just the twin spots of colour in her cheeks betraying her emotion. 'You're enjoying this, aren't you?' she spat, contemptuous eyes raking the good-looking figure lounging against the door-jamb. 'You've never liked me; never. Right from the start you disapproved, never thought me good enough for Danny, never wanted him to marry me. Well, it looks as if you've got your way. I don't know what you've said to turn him against me, but you've won, Luke Sinclair; you've won. Are you satisfied now?'

'What makes you think I had anything to do with it? Danny's a big boy, Celina. He makes his own decisions these days.'

'Oh, yes?' Her voice dripped sarcasm. 'Then why isn't he here? No—don't bother to tell me. I don't want any more lies. I already know the answer. I guess I've known all along. I just didn't want to believe it. Big brother raises his little finger and Danny goes running. Just as he always did. Just as he always will.'

'My dear,' Luke shrugged mockingly, 'you over-estimate my influence.'

'While you,' Celina hissed, 'insult my intelligence.'

There was a loaded pause, the moment two boxers facing each other from their respective corners weighed up the opposition, the fraction of a second before the bell galvanised them into action, when glances locked and psychology battled for advantage.

Unexpectedly Luke smiled, a strange, rueful, half-apologetic smile, and Celina's heart turned over. She had never stopped to analyse her feelings for Danny's handsome half-brother. It was enough that sparks had flown from the start, their mutual dislike flaring in-stantly, smouldering silently on. Nothing had been said, of course—Luke was much too clever for that—but the animosity was there, thinly concealed behind the mask of politeness, the veneer of cold but perfectly correct social behaviour. Now, facing him across the polished empty space of the register office waiting-room, Celina felt her world shift, her already confused emotions turn a somersault.

Anita's return broke the moment, her expression tight as she paused in the doorway, troubled eyes meeting Celina's. She shook her head slowly, almost impercep-tibly, and the faint flicker of hope inside Celina died. That was it, then. Probably as well really, common sense told her, had been telling her for weeks if she was honest. Danny was fun, a welcome ray of sunshine in her life, but she should have left it at that, shouldn't have al-lowed him to wear her down, should never have suc-cumbed to his persuasions. Marriage was far too serious a step to be taken with reservations. And yet it could have worked, it *would* have worked; Celina would have made it.

'It isn't good,' Anita told her softly, the unspoken sympathy in her eyes almost more than Celina could bear. 'Danny's gone abroad. The message on the Ansafone was short but succinct. He's gone to Europe, length of stay uncertain, and in the meantime any personal or business queries are directed to——'

'Luke Sinclair,' Celina interrupted drily. 'I'd never have guessed.' She lifted her chin automatically, her glance slipping past Anita, flicking over to Luke, who still hadn't moved, hands thrust into his pockets, supreme indifference oozing from every line of him. She swallowed her disappointment, the damage to her pride still raw, masking over the tiny *frisson* of relief. 'Come on,' she told Anita with a bright and brittle smile. 'Let's go. There's no point hanging around here; not any longer.'

She spun round, reaching for her handbag as Luke's voice brought her up sharp.

'Celina?'

Her head shot up. He had uncoiled himself from the doorpost and moved in behind her, the nearness of his body strangely unnerving.

'Luke?' she answered warily, colour flooding her cheeks and then ebbing away, leaving her entire face pale as fine bone china. She sensed Anita's presence at her side, hostility and indignation quivering on the air, but Celina flashed her another tight smile and the unspoken message passed between them.

'I'll wait downstairs,' Anita said, her eyes shooting daggers at Luke as she walked past. And then they were alone.

Silence. Not even the steady tick, tick, tick of a clock. Nothing intruding. No voice in the distance, just Celina's heart thumping in her breast, the sound echoing in her ears. She raised her eyes, finding his glance locked on her face, and instinctively she straightened her spine, squared her shoulders, and tossed him a glance of pure defiance.

'You've got guts,' he admitted grudgingly, admiringly, that strange smile playing about his mouth. 'I expected tears and tantrums, raving hysterics, not venom and ice-cool calm.'

The tears welled up again, the unexpected words touching a nerve. He was wrong. Very wrong. Her insides were in turmoil but she wouldn't give him the satisfaction of knowing. After today they'd probably never meet again. His world and hers were poles apart. Danny had opened a door but she was a fool to have imagined that she could ever cross the threshold. Still, she would go out fighting, an Oscar-winning performance designed to keep her pride intact.

'They breed us strong in the north,' she informed him matter-of-factly. 'Not simpering misses designed to acquiesce to a man's every whim. But it takes a strong man to hold us. That was my mistake. I thought Danny could do it, till you stepped in and proved otherwise. Still, perhaps you've done me a favour.'

'I *know* I have.' Luke stopped. He closed the gap between them, reaching out, long slender fingers gripping her shoulders, sending waves of heat coursing through her body. 'Listen, Celina,' he began urgently, mesmeric eyes holding hers, 'I need to talk to you. I've got something I want to ask. Can we go somewhere? Anywhere? For a coffee if you like. Give me ten minutes. If you don't like what I've got to say I'll walk out of your life and never bother you again.'

'It's a pity you ever walked into it,' Celina observed bitterly, twisting herself out of his grasp. 'Whatever it is, Luke, keep it to yourself. There's not a thing you can say that I could possibly want to hear. Let's not prolong the agony. You've had your money's worth today; let's just leave it at that.'

She turned away, picking up her bag, tucking the soft ivory leather under her arm. It was a perfect match for the suit she wore and she'd scoured the shops to find it, wincing visibly at the price. The entire outfit had cost a fortune, money she couldn't afford, money down the drain now. She could sell it, she supposed, but she'd still lose out. Second-hand clothes didn't exactly command top prices. She'd run an advert in the evening paper— 'Wedding outfit. One careful owner', perhaps, or, 'Off-white suit; suit off-white bride'. Her mouth twisted wryly.

'What's the matter?' Luke goaded, mistaking her expression. 'What are you afraid of? You're perfectly safe with me, Celina, especially in public.'

'Afraid?' she queried, halting in the doorway, tossing him a glance of pure disdain. 'Oh, no, Luke. I'm not afraid. Not of you, not of any man, not any more. But for once in my life I'm going to do exactly what *I* want to do. And making polite conversation with something that has just crawled out from underneath a stone simply doesn't appeal.'

She didn't wait for a reaction, just turned on her heels and walked calmly down the stairs, her outward appearance completely at odds with her churning insides. She smiled automatically as she passed a group of people on their way in, another happy couple about to tie the knot, she realised with a stab of pain.

'Now what?' Anita enquired as Celina drew level in the foyer.

Celina's voice was bleak. 'I suppose I should go round to Danny's. He may have left a letter or a message. But something tells me I'll be wasting my time.' She shrugged. 'There'll be nothing there. I'd put money on it. Luke's much too clever not to have out-guessed my reactions. But I'll go anyway, just in case. Miracles have been known to happen.' But even to her own ears the words didn't sound very convincing.

Anita's Mini was parked round the corner, but Celina slowed down as they approached it, her mind mulling over a range of possibilities. She hadn't planned the day, leaving it to Danny to arrange. 'Just surprise me,' she had told him, anticipating dinner at a top restaurant, tickets for a West End show, a honeymoon night in a plush hotel.

In other circumstances, Celina would have appreciated the irony of Danny's taking her at her word. But not today. She simply couldn't understand it. It wasn't like Danny at all. Light-hearted, easygoing, thoughtless on occasions, yes, but never cruel, never deliberately hurtful, never malicious. Too mindful of the brother he hero-worshipped, Celina decided, lips tightening at the thought. It had to be Luke's doing. Nothing else made sense. But what on earth had he said to Danny to send him off without an explanation today of all days?

Anita inserted her key in the lock as Celina reached a decision. 'You go home, Anita. I'll walk to Danny's. I've got a headache coming on and I need some fresh air. Besides, it's only ten minutes or so from here. I'll be all right,' she added, sensing her friend's start of surprise. 'After all, I'm hardly the classic jilted bride. I'll be fine. Honestly.'

Anita frowned. 'But I don't like leaving you like this, not now. Why not come back with me? I've nothing special planned. We could have lunch somewhere, or catch a film, or go shopping, or whatever you'd like to do. You must do *something*,' she urged, concern furrowing her brow.

Celina shook her head. 'Thanks, Anita, it's a nice idea and I'm almost tempted, but another day perhaps.'

'Tonight, then? You can't possibly stay in by yourself and mope. It's just not right.'

'You're going to worry yourself into a frazzle if I say no, aren't you?' Celina asked, but not unkindly. 'All right,' she smiled, 'I give in. Tonight it is.'

They arranged to meet at eight at a favourite pub, deliberately leaving plans for the evening open. Under the circumstances Celina would have preferred her own company, but perhaps Anita was right. She would only mope if left alone, even her sunny nature dampened by the day's events. Or, rather, non-events, she found herself correcting, standing on the pavement and eyeing the gathering clouds. Why hadn't she noticed before that it was going to rain? Her suit would ruin if she got it wet and that meant she'd better take a taxi. Another expense she'd much rather do without. And then she remembered. There was a bus she could catch just around the corner.

'Obviously not my lucky day,' she muttered two minutes later, halting in dismay as the familiar red bus drew away from the kerb and headed off into the distance.

Stirrings of self-pity began to insinuate themselves in her mind. She should have gone home with Anita, or taken that taxi, or stayed in bed, or done anything at all, in fact, apart from what she had done. She felt the first light patter of raindrops on her cheeks as tears of frustration pricked the backs of her eyes. Damn! Damn! Damn! Now she really would get soaked. And damn Luke Sinclair, she added, spotting a black cab cruising by and raising her hand in an effort to attract its attention. The taxi sailed past, leaving her stranded in the gutter, and her silent condemnation of Luke became even more vitriolic. It was all his fault, interfering in her life, manipulating Danny's, playing God for some twisted motive of his own. Young, rich, good-looking, arrogant Luke Sinclair.

Completely caught up in her misery, she didn't notice the silver Porsche pull in just ahead of her. It wasn't until she drew level that something familiar about the figure leaning nonchalantly against the car's bodywork made her turn her head. Her eyes locked with Luke's. Faint amusement mocked her. Colour flooded her cheeks and she stiffened at once.

'Are you following me?' she demanded coldly. 'If so, you're wasting your time.'

'Get in,' he ordered, ignoring her question as he threw open the passenger-door. She hesitated, and Luke's expression tightened. 'Don't be ridiculous, Celina,' he derided. 'You'll catch your death walking the streets dressed like that. It's going to pour down any minute. Catching pneumonia hardly makes sense, does it?'

For a full sixty seconds common sense battled against the overwhelming urge to march off down the road, leaving him stranded on the pavement. The patter of raindrops had begun to drum steadily on the roof of the car, had begun to seep through the thin material of her jacket. With an ill-concealed sigh Celina climbed in, fastening her seatbelt, fixing her eyes rigidly on the road ahead.

Luke didn't speak as he slipped in beside her, the powerful engine roaring into life, edging back into the stream of traffic. For five minutes no extra sound broke the silence, just the steady hum of the engine, the swish of the windscreen-wiper blades sweeping the glass in front of her. Celina tried to ignore him, but his presence at her side unnerved her.

'Where are we going?' she forced herself to ask. She had assumed he was taking her home and it simply didn't occur to her that Luke might have other ideas. But, as the car ate up the miles and the familiar streets were left behind, she began to feel uneasy.

'Relax, Celina,' Luke told her softly. 'As I said earlier, I simply want ten minutes of your time. You can spare me that, surely, in exchange for a lift home?'

'I don't seem to have much choice, do I?' she snapped, beginning to feel trapped and not liking the sensation one bit.

'Oh, I wouldn't say that,' he contradicted slyly. 'In fact, you're free to climb out of here whenever you want to. Shall I pull in at the lay-by, or can you force yourself to trust me?' He slowed down, watching Celina out of the corner of his eye. The rain was a steady stream by this time, the sky dark with reinforcements. Only an idiot would risk a soaking miles from home and inadequately dressed. Celina sighed. She'd been right in the first place: she didn't have much choice, and Luke knew it.

'Very well,' she acknowledged evenly, stifling her annoyance. 'You win, Luke, this time. I'm all yours for ten minutes, and ten minutes only.'

'Is that a promise?' he asked, turning his head towards her, smiling, unexpectedly teasing. 'Because if it is you could be giving more than you bargained for.'

'I doubt it,' Celina countered coldly. 'I doubt it very much.'

'Marry you? You're insane!'

'No, Celina. I'm perfectly sane, perfectly serious.'

'Perfectly serious? Don't make me laugh.' She gulped the rest of her coffee, the cup rattling in the saucer as she replaced it. 'This is your idea of a joke, isn't it?' she demanded, nostrils flaring slightly as she controlled her rising anger. 'Just like the rest of the day, in fact. Luke Sinclair's indulging his twisted sense of humour, insulting me, humiliating me, watching me squirm.'

'No, Celina,' he contradicted evenly, 'it isn't like that at all.'

'Don't lie, Luke; you're enjoying every moment. Why not be honest and admit it? It's a farce, and has been from the start. Danny and Celina, a music-hall turn. Well, how very amusing,' she sneered, arctic eyes ranging his face, blasting out her chill contempt. 'I haven't had so much fun in ages. *Do* remind me to do it again some time, won't you?'

Abruptly she pushed back her chair, rising to her feet, automatically reaching for her handbag. She nodded across at him dismissively. 'Thanks for the drink, Luke. I'm going. I'll see myself home.'

'Oh, no, you don't.' Luke's hand shot out, catching her off guard, his steely grip circling her wrist, trapping her. 'I haven't finished with you yet. You promised me ten minutes, remember, and by my reckoning there's another seven left. Sit down,' he added crisply, fingers relaxing their hold a little as he took her compliance for granted. 'Just hear me out. It won't take long.'

'You've got a nerve,' she spat, snatching her hand away, her features dark and thunderous. Just who did he think he was, ordering her about left, right and centre, arranging her life, organising Danny's? Interfering, manipulative, arrogantly all-knowing. She opened her mouth to speak, to tell him exactly what she thought of him, when unexpectedly Luke's whole expression lightened, and for the second time in the space of half an hour Celina's world turned upside-down.

'Sit down, Celina,' he repeated in a softer tone, intense blue eyes pinning her with their gaze, and then, softer still, a single word. 'Please.'

Like an obedient child, she sat, lowering her gaze, studying the pattern on the table-cloth as she struggled to pull herself together. She must have been mad accepting that lift. The morning had been difficult enough without putting herself back in the firing line, giving Luke more opportunities to gloat, to goad, to poke fun at her. She was all churned up inside and it was all his doing, blowing hot then cold, saying one thing, doing another, creating havoc. By now she should have been safely married to Danny, and instead here she was exchanging acid comments with the very man responsible for ruining all her plans.

'Why did you want to marry Danny?' Luke asked, once the waitress had cleared away the debris and brought them a fresh pot of coffee. 'You didn't love him, did you?'

'No.' She decided on the truth. It didn't matter any more, in any case. She hadn't loved Danny and he hadn't loved her. Yet they were suited, and in a strange sort of way they were good for each other, and they were friends. And Danny was her security—and, damn it, he'd stood her up!

Celina seethed inwardly. She didn't blame Danny, not one bit. He was just a pawn in his brother's game. No, she knew exactly who was responsible. Her stormy eyes ranged Luke's slouching form. He was leaning back in the chair, the picture of ease and composure, not the least put out by Celina's scowling mien and completely oblivious to the glances of admiration he was drawing from other women seated about the room.

Everything about him oozed money and quality, from the top of his golden head, hair worn slightly longer than was fashionable but so obviously expertly styled, to the tips of his toes, comfortably encased in the handmade soft leather shoes. And yet there was nothing showy or ostentatious about him. Just the aura of understated good taste.

'Danny was aware of my feelings,' she informed him coldly. 'I hadn't tricked or lied my way into his marriage bed. He knew exactly what he was letting himself in for, and, as you so pointedly told me earlier, he's a big boy now; he can stand on his own two feet, or he could till you poisoned his mind against me.'

Luke spread his hands expansively. 'Why should I want to interfere?' he asked mildly. 'You're a young and very beautiful woman, an asset to any man.'

'Any man but your brother,' she spat. 'Keep your backhanded compliments, Luke. They won't work, not with me. And I *know* you were responsible, so don't

bother to deny it. Danny might be impulsive, and in lots
of ways he's still very immature, but he would never
have humiliated me like this without your interference.
I hope you're proud of yourself, meddling cold-
bloodedly in other people's lives. It's despicable, *you're*
despicable, and if I live to be a hundred I'll never forgive
you for this; never.'

'I bet you won't.' Luke's voice was hard, ugly. 'Got
it all figured out, hadn't you, Celina? A meal-ticket for
life from my gullible little brother. I know your sort,
bleeding a man dry, drop by drop, taking everything he
has, taking, taking, always taking, squeezing the very
soul from his body. But not this time, Celina. Not Danny.
You'll have to find yourself another rich mug to marry
because Danny's not interested any more.' He looked
her up and down, thinly veiled contempt sweeping the
length of her. 'You're young, you're pretty and you've
got a good body. I'm sure you'll have no trouble selling
yourself to another high bidder.'

'Like yourself, perhaps?' she demanded icily, matching
his contempt with a brand of her own. 'That *was* your
proposal, wasn't it, Luke, not ten minutes since? How
could you even stoop to think of it?' she jeered, gathering her gloves and bag and pushing back her chair with
slow, considered movements that were completely at odds
with her seething insides. She met his glance full on, her
own eyes scornful. 'If you were the last man on this
earth, Luke, the answer would still be the same. Thanks,
but no thanks; I'm really not that hard up.'

'Why?'

Celina laughed, a harsh, grating sound which echoed
round the room, halting conversations, turning curious
heads in their direction. 'You couldn't even begin to
understand,' she told him witheringly. 'And now, if
you'll excuse me, I've better things to do with my time.'

She reached the door before she realised that Luke
was right behind her. She carried on walking, ignoring

his presence—or trying to. It was difficult marching down the street in the pouring rain, trying to hang on to her dignity with the cause of her humiliation hot on her heels, matching her stride for stride.

'Go away,' she spat. 'Leave me alone.'

She increased her pace, dashing across the road, dodging the horn-blaring traffic which had to swerve to avoid her. She hadn't a clue where she was going. Blindly she walked on, rain quickly soaking through the thin material of her suit, plastering her long dark hair against her head and shoulders. She grew chilled, but still she pushed herself on, never glancing to right nor left, head held high, back ramrod straight.

Finally she slowed down. Glancing surreptitiously into shop windows, she satisfied herself that none of the murky reflections showed Luke's six-foot-two-inch form, and she allowed herself to relax a little.

A taxi pulled up, disgorging its passengers, and Celina dashed forwards before it could take off. Shivering visibly, she climbed into a corner, glad to be out of the rain. She'd go home. Danny's could wait. If there was a message—*if*, she added sceptically—it would still be there in an hour or so, a day or so. The urgency had gone. In any case, deep down she knew what she'd find when she got there: nothing, nothing at all.

Pushing open the communal front door and stepping over the threshold, Celina breathed a weary sigh. She was home and she was safe. And then a familiar figure moved in the gloom, swimming into focus.

'I should have known. Ten out of ten for persistence, Luke.' She made to brush past, heading for the stairs, but he forestalled her, blocking her way.

'I think we've some unfinished business to discuss.'

'And I think not. Let me past, Luke. I'm cold and I'm wet through and I'm thoroughly fed up.'

They stood for a moment, face to face, eyes locked, the expression in both grim.

Celina broke the deadlock with another heavy sigh. 'Oh, very well,' she muttered with ill-concealed reluctance. 'You'd better come up.'

She led the way, painfully aware of the shabby, unswept carpet, the cloying odour of stale cabbage that seemed a permanent part of the house's atmosphere. The solid Victorian villa, once the home of a prosperous middle-class family, had fallen into disrepair over the years. The whole neighbourhood had seen better days, and most of the buildings, like this one, had been converted into bedsits and flats.

She let herself into her tiny top-floor flat. 'Sit down,' she told him curtly as she put a match to the portable gas heater. 'I'll put the kettle on and then I'll get changed. I'll be five minutes. Do make yourself at home,' she ended with more than a hint of sarcasm, before disappearing into the kitchen.

She took her time, aware at the back of her mind that she was stalling, giving herself breathing-space, postponing the moment when she went back to face him. She was suddenly afraid, and she didn't know why except that it was all tied up with Luke somehow. They'd always been antagonistic, but today the hostility was tempered with a new emotion, one equally raw but which refused her attempts at identification.

She towelled her hair, rubbing warmth back into her numb body before scanning the rails in the wardrobe for something to wear. What she wanted was a hot bath, a long, luxurious soak with a stiff vodka and tonic and the company of a good book, but the immersion wasn't programmed to come on for another hour, and glasses of spirits were expensive little extras she had made herself forgo for some time now.

Pulling on a warm woollen dress, she paused in front of the mirror. The deep red suited her, matching the glints in the long dark hair. Irish colouring, Danny had called it, teasing her, and thinking of Danny dragged her thoughts back to Luke. She stiffened. She'd have to face him sooner or later; it might as well be now.

'Quite a collection of books you've got here.' He was standing in front of a bookcase and didn't turn round when Celina entered the small but cheerful sitting-room carrying a tray of drinks and biscuits. 'Cosmopolitan taste, too.' He ran his fingers along a shelf, bringing out a slim volume of poetry. '"The orchards half the way from home to Ludlow fair, flowered on the first of May in Mays when I was there,"' he quoted as the book fell open at its most worn page. 'You do continue to surprise me.'

'What did you expect?' she enquired, feeling the blood rush to her cheeks at the unexpected comments. 'Penny Dreadfuls? Real-life romance? I just love books. If I were desperate enough I think I'd even re-read Noddy.'

'Yes, but why Housman? Why not Donne or Betjeman, or someone modern? Ted Hughes perhaps. Housman's not exactly in vogue at the moment.'

'I like Housman.' Celina sat down abruptly, to all intents and purposes closing the subject. He couldn't know it, but Luke had touched a nerve. The book had been a present from her father, and just now thoughts about her father, on top of everything else, would be the last straw.

She hugged her coffee-mug, drawing on its warmth, watching as he replaced the book and seated himself opposite. He lounged on the settee, perfectly at ease in her minuscule sitting-room.

Celina had made the most of the room. A single window dominated an entire wall and she had shunned curtains in favour of a paper blind which allowed the sun, on days it chose to shine, to filter through, delicate fingers of light casting their golden glow. The walls had been painted a bright and beaming yellow, so that even on dismal days, like this one, the room retained a cheery ambience. Pot-plants abounded, some grouped on low tables and on the floor, others hanging from the ceiling. Pride of place, though, went to her collection of books, as Luke had so rightly identified, a cosmopolitan feast created for a mind hungry for words, knowledge or just plain entertainment.

'Well?' she asked, pushing a plateful of biscuits across the coffee-table towards him.

'It's very simple. I want you to marry me.' He was watching her intently, but Celina couldn't decipher the expression in his eyes.

As in the coffee-shop, she heard herself exclaim, 'You're mad! Besides, we've been over that already. I don't know what your game is, but you can definitely count me out. You're wasting your time. It isn't even funny any more. Go home, Luke. I've had enough of your twisted sense of humour for one day.'

'You're wrong, Celina. I've never been more serious in my life. Why don't you let me explain?'

'What's there to explain? You've never liked me, never considered me good enough for Danny, and, if I'm not good enough for him, how could I possibly measure up to standard for his fastidious brother? No, you're laughing at me, dangling a carrot for some devious motive of your own. The moment I say yes you'll throw it all back in my face and make me feel even smaller than I already do. I've had my snub today, Luke. Isn't that enough? You don't have to rub my nose in it, surely?'

'You're wrong,' he repeated. 'You don't understand.' He replaced the cup on the table and leaned forwards, the lines of his body tense and urgent. 'I'm not asking for a conventional marriage. Good Lord, Celina, there's half a dozen women who'd happily swoon into my arms tomorrow if I so much as hinted at the idea——'

'Well, then, ask one of them,' she interrupted pertly.

'And be lumbered for years with some empty-headed bimbo who'd take me for every penny I've got in a divorce settlement? No, Celina. I want a marriage of convenience. I want a woman with more than a grain of sense, who'll allow me the freedom to go my own way, live my own life. I want a woman who'll look good at my side when I'm entertaining; a woman I can take with pride to the theatre, the ballet, the opera; a woman other men will envy me for and, more importantly, who will understand when Miss Right comes along and will step aside without any fuss and fade away into the background. I want *you*.'

'You really have got a nerve!' Celina spluttered, too stunned to be angry. She wanted to tear her gaze away, to sever the alarming, mesmeric contact. As Luke had warmed to his subject his face had come alive, the usually steely eyes glinting with enthusiasm, his whole expression softening the angle of his jaw. He had never looked more attractive than he did now, blond waves rippling on his collar, the expectant smile hovering about the generous lips, the blue, oh, so blue eyes dancing with lights. Illogically she found herself wondering how she had managed to miss the sapphire depths in the dark-fringed eyes, how she had ever thought the clear-cut lines of his face cold and cruel. Even more illogically, she felt herself imagining the strength of his arms as he held her close, the tender probings of his mouth as he kissed her...

She pulled her thoughts up sharp, appalled at the powerful stab of emotion that sent her senses reeling. Jumping up in agitation, she moved over to the window, raising the blind so that she could lean on the windowsill, pull herself together.

What Luke was suggesting was outrageous, totally out of the question, and yet was it really any different from Danny's proposal? Yes! she screamed silently, resting her throbbing head on the cool pane of glass. The two suggestions simply didn't compare. The reasons were different, vastly different, the motives poles apart. Danny had wanted *her*, not some mannequin to trot out and perform in front of guests, to be pushed into the background when no longer required. And, if it hadn't seemed like the stuff of grand romance, it had been enough for Danny, more than enough for Celina. No, Luke wanted something else entirely. The whole idea was preposterous. And yet, a tiny voice inside her head was saying, it was an answer, in a way. How easy it would be to say yes, and how impossible too. She shook her head.

'You haven't said no anyway; at least not yet.'

Celina turned slightly. Luke was at her side, still watching her carefully. 'You can't possibly be serious,' she told him once she was sure her voice was under control. 'You've already lumped me with your contemptible breed, a gold-digger, a fortune-hunter, an empty-headed bimbo. What's to stop me saying yes and then doing exactly what you're afraid of—taking you for a ride, taking you for every penny? No, Luke, it's a stupid idea, and the answer's still the same. No, I will not marry you.'

'But you would have married Danny?'

'What's that got to do with it?'

'Everything—and nothing. It's the same principle. You didn't love Danny, yet you wanted to marry him. You don't love me, but you refuse even to consider a serious business proposition. I'm offering you a job, Celina, nothing more, nothing less. A fixed-term contract to be terminated on request, your request if that's what you want. I can afford to give you everything that Danny could. Marry me, Celina; marry me instead.'

'No.'

'Why?'

'You wouldn't understand.'

'Try me.'

'No.' Celina turned back to the view.

'Look at me, damn you!' Luke spun her round, the touch of his fingers on her arms electrifying, shocking in intensity. As Celina felt her body begin to tremble she forced herself to breathe deep and long.

She couldn't do it. She wasn't sure of her reasons, but she could never marry Luke, never. And yet, without Danny, there was so much she was going to lose, and not only for herself. She started to waver, almost allowing herself to be persuaded, but no! She mustn't. She couldn't, she wouldn't allow herself to weaken, despite the mounting pressure.

Luke's hands continued to hold her, an iron grip on her upper arms. Celina pulled away, attempting to wriggle free, but the more she struggled, the deeper the fingers bit into her flesh. With a huge effort of will she forced herself to relax, Luke's rigid hold loosening almost imperceptibly.

'Tell me,' he insisted, steely eyes boring into hers. 'Do tell me, Celina. What exactly does Danny have that I can't give you? After all, you *were* marrying him for his money, not for his good looks and his lashings of charm. I'm intrigued. You're the most unusual fortune-hunter I've ever encountered. You obviously wanted the money badly enough to marry him, and yet, when I can give you everything that he could, you turn me down flat. What is it?' he asked, his face only inches away from hers. 'Still hoping he'll come running?' He laughed, an ugly sneer crossing his face. 'Forget it, Celina. You've lost him. But don't take my word for it, give him a ring. Yes, go ahead; I'll even dial the number for you.'

He dragged her across the room, releasing one arm as he reached the phone. He placed the receiver on the coffee-table and Celina watched with awful fascination as he slowly dialled the number she knew so well.

'No!' She heard the connection made and slammed her free hand down on the cradle. She couldn't bear it, not listening to the disembodied tones of Danny's recorded message, not with Luke at her side, hardly bothering to conceal his gloating satisfaction.

'No?' he enquired, raising a quizzical eyebrow. 'Dear me. Don't you want to sort it out, Celina? There's got to be a reason, a perfectly logical explanation. After all, it's not every day that the bride's left standing at the altar, as it were.' He brought his head closer, lips curling in derision, eyes full of scorn, voice oozing contempt. 'And you have been running after Danny for quite some time now, haven't you, Celina? Why waste all that energy, all that hard work? Why stop running now when there's so much at stake, when you're so close to your conquest?'

Celina reacted instinctively, jerking free of his grasp and hitting out, her right hand delivering a stinging blow to the side of his cheek. Appalled, she could only stand and watch as the imprint of her fingers turned first white then red.

'Well, well, well,' he murmured, rubbing his cheek with the back of his hand. 'So the lady has spirit. I wonder if Danny knows just what a jewel he's letting slip through his fingers? A veritable firebrand, no less; a gutsy, strong-willed, stubborn, but very beautiful firebrand. Well, I guess I asked for that one, but before I go—and yes, I really am going this time; I think I've got the message—just for the record, tell me: why Danny? Why not me?'

'It's perfectly simple, Luke. I *like* Danny.'

'I see.'

For a fleeting moment Celina was conscious that she'd hurt him. She felt the pain run through her. She hadn't meant to hurt, merely to explain. She wanted to step forwards, to tell him she was sorry. There was enough pain in the world already without her causing more. She opened her mouth to speak but bit off the comment as Luke's mouth hardened into a grim line. How foolish, she mocked silently, her insides turning to stone. As if she could possibly hurt someone as arrogant as Luke

Sinclair. He wasn't bred for hurt. He wouldn't recognise it if it hit him in the face!

He turned away, heading for the door, and through a blur of tears Celina followed. A buff envelope lay on the mat. It must have been there earlier and gone unnoticed on their arrival. Luke stooped and picked it up, silently holding it out for Celina to take. She recognised the crest on the back immediately and her heart sank.

Luke's glance flicked over her, interested for a moment and then cold again. He opened the door, stepping out on to the landing.

'Don't bother to see me out,' he told her curtly, dismissively. 'I'm sure you've more important things demanding your attention. Goodbye, Celina.'

And he set off down the stairs, his words hanging in the air, chilling Celina with their ring of finality. She could only stand on the shabby landing, listening to his footsteps, hugging the envelope to her chest, her thoughts a churning, sickening confusion, until a door slammed in the distance and her straining ears could hear no more. And the silence, once he had gone, was deafening.

CHAPTER TWO

THE letter, as Celina had expected, was not good news. The Kingsmead Nursing Home regretted very much that its fees were having to rise, but in the present economic climate the move was unavoidable. The timing, given the disasters of the rest of the day, couldn't have been worse.

It hadn't been easy for Celina, battling to make ends meet, scrimping and scraping, making do with little for herself, regularly doing without the things other women her age took for granted: a new lipstick, a spare pair of tights, a salon cut and blow dry. But she'd done it and done it willingly. She'd done it for her father. And it was only when the struggle had begun to wear her down, when the money in her wage-cheque at the end of each month had begun to be inadequate to cover living expenses, the nursing-home bills and her other self-imposed repayments that Celina had allowed herself to be persuaded by Danny.

He had been like a breath of fresh air in her life, full of fun, full of laughter, and almost from the moment they'd met he'd urged Celina to marry him. If he'd proposed once he'd proposed a dozen times, often in the most incongruous of circumstances, on one memorable occasion getting down on his knees in the middle of Regent Street, bringing traffic to a halt as Celina had laughingly pleaded with him to get out of the way.

And always she'd said no, recognising instinctively that, though he'd professed to love her, Danny was in love with the idea, that part of his reason at least was a subconscious desire to impress his older brother.

Finally, after months and months of urgings and cajolings, Celina surprised herself one night by saying yes. She'd supposed later that Danny had caught her on the raw. She'd spent her afternoon off at the nursing home, but it had been a complete waste of time. Her father hadn't recognised her at all, barely acknowledging that he even had a visitor. She'd spent many afternoons like that, of course, but somehow that day everything had seemed so futile, so soul-destroying, so damned unfair.

Arriving home to find Danny camped on her doorstep was just the fillip Celina had needed. Her spirits had soared at once and the nightmare afternoon had, for an hour or two, faded into the background. They'd gone out to a club, the noisy music and lively atmosphere keeping unwanted thoughts at bay but, even so, agreeing to another of Danny's proposals was the last thing Celina had intended. Until they'd headed for home, stepped out into the cold night air and stumbled on the crowd of people huddled round the unconscious form of the old man on the pavement. The ambulance had pulled up to the whispered diagnoses rippling round the curious onlookers. 'Had one too many,' someone had stated, over-loudly. 'No, heart attack. Can tell from the colour of him,' someone else had proclaimed. But it was the last suggestion that had hit home with Celina. Just the one word: 'Stroke.'

She'd almost broken down, but had swallowed her tears, had sat in silence beside Danny as he'd whisked her home, hadn't been able to separate the picture of the old man lying inert on the pavement from the picture of her father in the cold white hospital ward on the morning he'd been taken in.

And when Danny had repeated his proposal some half-hour later, Celina had agreed, almost without thinking, subconsciously seeking to inject a little happiness into her life, reaching out for some tangible proof that things would get better, that her father would improve, that the future would be something to look forward to.

Strange, really, how she hadn't confided in Danny even then. Fun-loving Danny, never serious for a moment. She'd had the ideal opportunity and yet she'd let it pass. Intuition perhaps?

The phone rang, startling Celina, whose blood ran hot then cold, and she dropped the letter, watching with curious detachment as the flimsy piece of paper fluttered to the floor. She bent to retrieve it and then reached for the receiver, a shiver of apprehension running the length of her. Danny, apologising perhaps? Luke, gloating? Or, worse, the nursing home with unwelcome news?

'Anita!' Relief and disappointment both, though quite why the latter she didn't stop to analyse.

'Just checking you got home all right,' Anita's voice trilled down the phone line. 'It started to pour down just after I left you, but, by the time I'd negotiated the one-way system to get back to you, you'd gone. Did you get very wet?' she asked, and then laughed at the absurdity of the question.

Celina set her mind at rest. 'I came home by taxi,' she explained, leaving out Luke's role in the proceedings. Time enough to recount that later.

They chatted on for a few more minutes, Anita clearly wishing to reassure herself that Celina was all right, and Celina suffered patiently the gentle probings about her welfare, allowing herself to smile at the image she conjured up of a mother hen clucking about her brood.

To fill the remainder of the afternoon Celina unpacked the small suitcase that had stood ready in her bedroom. It was easier than she'd expected, and, now that the decision had been taken out of her hands, she found herself relaxing. Danny had gone. It still hurt that he'd let her down, left her wide open to other people's scorn or pity, but that would fade in time, she realised, and in the meantime the threads of relief that had started to surface were firmly squashed, pushed back into her subconscious, Celina's heart not yet ready to face up to their wider implications.

She went back to work on Monday, having rung the department-leader beforehand and explained the position. She was lucky. Half the staff were down with flu, and so she had little time for idle thoughts. The library was open ten hours a day, six days a week, and having to work the extra hours to combat staff-shortages suited Celina down to the ground. And, on a purely practical level, the extra money was a godsend.

'How about a night out?' Anita suggested just over a week later. The two women were taking their afternoon tea-break and had the staff-room to themselves.

'Anywhere special in mind?' Celina asked, helping herself to a biscuit from the half-eaten packet on the table in front of her.

'Whimsies. That new club I told you about. I've been given a couple of complimentary tickets and thought we could drop in for an hour or two, see what it's like.'

'And what's happened to Zac?' Celina queried, referring to the latest in a long line of Anita's short-lived boyfriends.

'Out of town,' Anita informed her, pouring them both another cup of tea and draining the pot in the process. 'On business. Not that I'm sorry,' she confessed, adding milk and sugar to both and pushing Celina's cup back across the table.

'Oh?' Celina asked, swallowing a smile, recognising what was coming next. He'd be 'too possessive', or 'too intense', or 'much too serious', for Anita's easygoing disposition.

'He's simply no fun any more,' Anita explained as Celina turned her head away. 'He thinks he's in love. Wants us to get married. Married? Me! Honestly, Celina, can you imagine it?'

Celina couldn't, but she held her tongue, marriage not being one of the subjects she felt like discussing just yet, and instead turned the subject back to the evening ahead, finding herself agreeing to Anita's suggestion and spending the rest of the afternoon actually looking forward to going somewhere new.

She was humming lightly to herself as she ran down the steps at five o'clock, glad she wasn't working through till seven, and didn't notice the car parked opposite.

It had grown chilly, and Celina turned her collar up before dashing across the road, dodging the heavy traffic and almost careering full-tilt into a man waiting to cross in the opposite direction.

'I'm so sorry,' she murmured, hardly glancing up, and then she halted, stunned. 'Luke!' she exclaimed, the colour flaring in her cheeks as their eyes met.

'Celina,' he replied, the merest hint of a smile on his face.

'Lost your way?' she asked with heavy sarcasm, unable to think of a single reason why he should materialise in this particular area of London at the exact moment she was leaving work. Unless, of course, he intended taking up where he'd left off ten days earlier, baiting her, berating her.

'Not at all,' he replied smoothly. 'If you knew me better, Celina, you'd realise that I'm never lost. I always know exactly where I am and exactly where I'm going.'

'Lucky for you,' she retorted, attempting to slip past but foiled by Luke's neat sidestep.

'Going home?' he asked as Celina's head shot up in challenge.

'None of your business,' she bit out coldly, her eyes flashing ice.

'I could be going your way,' he suggested as she tried pushing past on his left side, only to be brought up sharp by Luke's substantial form.

'What's the matter?' she goaded, unable to shake him off and forced to stand and shiver on the pavement. 'Nobody to taunt, nobody to dominate with Danny out of the country? Go buy yourself another plaything, Luke. I'm sure you can afford it. And then perhaps you'd do me a favour and leave me alone.'

Luke merely shrugged, stepping aside, allowing Celina to brush past, her high heels echoing on the paving-stones as she attempted to put some distance between them. Reaching the end of the block, she allowed herself a backwards glance. Luke hadn't moved, his eyes meeting hers for a fleeting moment, and Celina flushed again, glad he wasn't near enough to notice. With a disdainful flick of her head she rounded the corner.

She half expected he'd be there again the following evening, but he wasn't, and as she swallowed the absurd twinge of disappointment she was forced to accept that Luke's appearance in the first place was probably pure coincidence. He was a businessman, after all, intent on making a living, and bumping into Celina had probably been as much of a surprise to him as it had been to her. Only Luke had been forewarned, had spotted Celina hurrying down the steps, had deliberately played the advantage when Celina had almost hurtled into his arms.

Consequently, Thursday lunchtime came as a bit of a shock. It was her half-day off, her afternoon for the nursing home, and, preoccupied with thoughts about her father, she didn't realise that her eyes were unconsciously seeking out Luke's distinctive form, didn't realise till her heart took a curious leap in her breast as she paused in the open doorway, hardly daring to believe what she was seeing.

'Bored, Luke?' she needled, forcing herself to follow her usual routine across the road, round the corner, down into the underground and safety. This time, to her dismay, he fell into step beside her.

'Come and have some lunch,' he said, ignoring her taunt as his easy stride kept pace with Celina's hurrying footsteps.

'It would choke me,' she retorted crisply and doing her best to ignore his presence at her side as she wove her way through the lunchtime crowds.

She reached the entrance to the tube station and didn't pause at all, turning in automatically, season-ticket in hand as she reached the turnstiles, relaxing slightly as the moving stairway carried her swiftly down into the subterranean network of arteries and veins that criss-crossed the city, pulsing with its human cargo.

The rumble of the train increased as Celina reached the platform and she stepped forwards, jostling for position as the whoosh of air that heralded the train's arrival lifted strands of her long dark hair off her shoulders. She surged forwards with the crowd, only to be brought up sharp by an iron grip on her arm.

'What the——?' She spun round, eyes shooting flames, her mouth tightening into a thin, angry line as she found herself face to face with Luke again. 'What the hell do you think you're doing?' she spat, tugging herself free but making no effort to resume her journey.

'Would you believe trying to have a conversation with the stubbornest creature on God's earth, she-ass excepted, of course.'

'Why?' she demanded, not a bit impressed by his easy manner, his ready smile.

'Come and have lunch and I'll explain,' he offered.

'I'm afraid I can't, Luke. Even if I wanted to. My diary for today is all full up. Poor you,' she mocked, watching with interest the momentary flash of anger which Luke controlled so swiftly that she wasn't sure later hadn't been her own imagination.

'Tomorrow, then? Or Saturday. Or is your social calendar much too crowded to spare me an hour or two?'

'Ah,' Celina purred, tilting back her head and meeting his gaze full on. 'I do believe you're beginning to get the message. And here's me, thinking you're much too thick-skinned to take a gentle hint.'

'Sarcasm doesn't become you,' he countered with perfect equanimity. 'Well?'

'You're going to carry on badgering me until I give in, aren't you?' Celina asked, beginning to enjoy their battle of words.

'I always knew your intelligence was wasted on Danny,' he observed.

'Now who's being sarcastic?' Celina flashed. Then, 'Leave Danny out of this.'

'Eight o'clock tomorrow, then? I'll pick you up.'

'I must be mad,' Celina muttered half under her breath as another train rumbled into view. She timed her moment well, darting away from Luke and leaping into the carriage as the automatic doors began to close, leaving him stranded on the platform.

He raised a lazy hand as the train zoomed off into the darkness, and Celina slumped thankfully into an empty seat, conscious that she might not have agreed to his absurd suggestion but that she hadn't said no either. And to a man like Luke that could only be taken as a sign of encouragement. Eight o'clock tomorrow. She shivered, though with cold or anticipation she couldn't quite be sure.

'How was your father?' Anita asked the following morning during a lull. They were working together, checking a recent delivery of new books, cross-referencing them against the order sheet and the delivery notes and putting them into sections on the stock-room shelves.

'About the same as last week,' Celina told her, pausing for a moment, her thoughts slipping back to the afternoon visit which had followed the same pattern as most weeks, her father in his wheelchair, lethargic, barely recognising her, Celina chatting on about anything and everything in an effort to engage his attention, trigger off some distant memory. Week after week after week she could sit there, her spirits sinking lower and lower until she reached the conclusion she was wasting her time. He couldn't hear her; he never would. And just as she'd inwardly accepted that he'd never improve she'd arrive one afternoon to find him cheerful and cognisant, and all the futile weeks that had gone before would be forgotten.

Anita flashed her a sympathetic glance. 'I don't know how you can bear it every Thursday afternoon. I don't think I'd be so selfless, giving up my free time so cheerfully, having to cope with all the disappointments. Life's not exactly fair on occasions, is it?' she asked, and Celina knew instinctively that her friend's thoughts had moved on from her father, had settled on Danny.

'I had a letter this morning,' Celina confided quietly.

'From Danny?' Anita's voice hardened. 'Full of excuses, I suppose. He always did have a silver tongue.'

'You didn't like him?' Celina commented, her tone half-query, half-statement.

Anita's eyebrows rose. 'I didn't *dislike* Danny,' she told her. 'I can't imagine anyone who could. But that's just the point. He's so easygoing, so likeable, so obliging, so—oh, I don't know, so *nice*, I suppose,' she added, shrugging her shoulders. 'Too nice. Too good to be true. And he did let you down,' she ended defensively as Celina's eyebrows rose in turn.

'He did have his arm twisted,' Celina felt obliged to point out.

'Humph,' Anita derided. 'I'll bet. So what did he have to say for himself?'

'That's what's so strange,' Celina replied, reaching for the scissors to open the next consignment of books. 'He didn't really say anything. It was almost as if he expected me to know why he didn't turn up.'

'In other words, he left big brother to break the un-welcome news. How considerate.'

'No. Not at all. But that's my point entirely. It was so out of character. Can't you see?' she asked, pausing for a moment, scissors in hand, hand in mid-air, head on one side, as she attempted to put her thoughts into words. 'Danny *was* considerate—and kind, and nice. You've just finished telling me how nice. He wouldn't take off without a word of explanation, not on our wedding-day.'

'But he did,' Anita pointed out softly, her stormy eyes clouding in concern as they rested on her friend.

'Exactly.'

Anita whistled under her breath. 'Luke?'

Celina nodded. 'Luke. It has to be. It's the only thing that makes any sense.'

They lapsed into silence, Anita seeming to recognise Celina's need to mull over her thoughts, Celina herself trying to view things objectively, her mind picking up ideas, chewing them over, discarding the more unlikely ones, coming back time and again to Luke. He hadn't told her the truth—that much was obvious. Danny had left a message, verbal or written, she didn't know which, but Luke had chosen not to pass it on, had openly sneered at Danny's defection, hadn't cared that Celina might be hurt and embarrassed. And then, to add insult to injury, Luke had made his own strange proposal.

She sighed, deciding that the more she tried, the less sense she seemed to make of it all, and worked on auto-matically, allowing her thoughts to drift, till by the end of the morning she'd made up her mind about one thing: she wanted the truth and she'd have the truth. And, since Danny couldn't provide it, it was all down to Luke. Sud-denly she was glad she was seeing him that evening. It gave her the chance to prepare her thoughts, to catch

Luke off guard. She smiled grimly. If Luke expected a nice, quiet evening, he was going to be very disappointed.

Luke raised his glass. 'To a pleasant evening,' he toasted, his glance locking with Celina's.

'If you say so,' she countered coldly before sipping her vodka and tonic.

The clear blue eyes narrowed dangerously, but any comment he might have made Luke kept to himself.

Surreptitiously she watched him from underneath her lashes. She felt out of place in the lush surroundings of the night-club, under-dressed, lacking in poise, downright gauche. And yet it wasn't the choice of venue that unnerved her. It was the company.

Luke sat back in his chair, perfectly relaxed, obviously at home, plainly determined not to let Celina's comments affect him. And why should they? Hadn't Luke the upper hand, choosing the time and place and the topic of conversation? He was in familiar territory and it showed. He oozed confidence, every inch of him proclaiming to the world that here was a successful man, a man of means, a man of power. The open-necked shirt that accompanied the expensive beige linen suit merely served to underline his indifference to public opinion, his complete disregard for convention. Luke Sinclair did what he wanted to do, his entire mien declared, and, most importantly, he did it his way.

'What is it that you want, Luke?' Celina asked abruptly, deciding it was time someone else took the initiative.

'Why should I *want* anything?' he queried with an easy smile that didn't fool Celina one iota. He wanted something all right, she'd put money on it. Why else would a man like him waste time on someone he despised?

'Don't tell me I've misjudged you,' she observed, her tone deceptively bland.

'Stranger things have happened,' Luke replied drily.

Celina inclined her head. 'True. But in this case, Luke, I think not.'

'Oh? Any particular reason for such damning conviction?' he enquired, mouth curved in mocking semblance of a smile.

'Danny.'

'Danny? And how do you work that one out? Danny's three hundred miles away.'

'Exactly,' Celina replied.

'So?'

'So this is the twentieth century, Luke. Distance is no longer any hindrance to communications. We've invented cunning little gadgets that enable people to send messages at the touch of a button.'

'The hell we have!' Luke bit out, suddenly alert, leaning forwards, the lines of his body taut with urgency. 'And what has Danny been saying, Celina? Do tell, my dear. I'm sure his comments must be worth repeating.'

'But that's just the point,' Celina replied, watching him carefully over the rim of her glass. 'Danny didn't *say* anything. He seemed to be suffering under the misapprehension that I'd already been told why he let me down. Why did he let me down, Luke? And I'd like the real reason this time, not your twisted version of it.'

'Why didn't you ask Danny yourself?' Luke retorted, reaching for his drink, draining the contents in one gulp and signalling the waiter for a refill.

'A little difficult without a return address,' Celina replied acidly.

Luke frowned. 'You mean Danny *wrote* to you?' he asked, seeming puzzled.

'Isn't that what I've been saying?' Celina snapped, barely controlling her irritation and missing completely the tension draining away from Luke's face as her words sank in.

He leaned back into the cushions. 'And?'

'And nothing. Nothing at all, so you tell me.'

Luke shrugged. 'As I told you on the day, Celina, Danny simply changed his mind. But that's Danny all over, too easygoing for his own good at times. Don't tell me you've never noticed his tendency to take the line of least resistance?'

'Helped along on this particular one by a not-so-gentle shove from older brother perhaps?'

Luke spread his hands expansively. 'You're not going to believe anything I say, Celina, so why should I bother even trying to convince you?'

'For once, Luke, you've hit the nail right on the head. You're hiding something, I know you are, and once Danny comes back I'm going to find out exactly what.'

'*If* Danny comes back,' Luke slipped in deceptively softly.

'Meaning?' Celina almost spat.

Luke shrugged. 'Out of sight, out of mind. Hard though it might be for you to accept the unpalatable, Danny's been in this position before. Ah, that's news, isn't it?' he almost purred, sensing Celina's start of surprise. 'Sorry to have to shatter your illusions, Celina, but you're just the latest in a long line of beautiful women who've set their caps at my gullible little brother.'

'You're lying.'

A single eyebrow rose. 'If you say so,' he mocked cruelly, his voice catching exactly Celina's earlier icy inflexion.

Colour flooded her cheeks. 'I do,' she spat, hanging on to her temper with a huge effort of will. 'And if Danny himself were to walk through that door now, a woman on each arm and another in tow, I still wouldn't believe your vile insinuations.'

'Such trust, such faith, such blind naïveté,' he taunted softly as the waiter returned with their drinks.

Celina seethed silently while the empty glasses were taken away and fresh ones set before them. It wasn't going quite as she'd envisaged, Luke seeming to have the upper hand, and she had the sneaking suspicion that he was deliberately goading, pushing, challenging— testing her almost. He wanted her to blow, she could see it all now, and in that case she was damned if she'd be so obliging.

She took a leaf from his book, forcing herself to sink back into the cushions, picking up her glass and cradling it, taking occasional sips as she made herself relax, banished the hard expression from her mouth.

'Jealous, Luke?' she asked sweetly, determined that the insults wouldn't slip by unchallenged.

'Of Danny? Should I be?' he queried, not a bit surprised at her change in attitude.

Celina made a pretence of thinking the question over. 'It takes a good man to generate loyalty,' she informed him. 'But do go ahead and sneer, it's cheap enough, and can't hurt Danny or me.'

'No, I think I'm beginning to agree with you there.' He leaned forwards, placing his glass on the table, his eyes no longer mocking as they met and held her own. 'But Danny's a fool, Celina. He's gone. He's left you. Whatever the reasons, the facts remain. He didn't want to marry you. If he did, nothing on this earth would have dragged him away. Don't you see? He doesn't deserve your loyalty. He doesn't deserve you.'

Celina laughed, throwing back her head, the auburn glints in her rich dark hair catching the light as the waves cascaded over her shoulders.

'You can't run with the hare and hunt with the hounds,' she admonished with mock-severity. Thank goodness she'd kept her sense of humour. How else could she deal with a man of so many different facets, a man who ruthlessly manipulated whatever situation presented itself, who'd already told her in no uncertain terms that she was little better than a gold-digger, but who now had the temerity to suggest that *Danny* wasn't good enough for *her*? She watched as Luke's expression softened, his mouth curving into a broad smile as he acknowledged the truth of Celina's gentle reprimand.

'So I changed my mind.' He shrugged easily, white teeth gleaming and even. 'It's not the exclusive prerogative of the female sex, and I'm man enough to admit when I'm wrong.'

'Well, well,' Celina trilled softly. 'I do believe that this time, Luke Sinclair, you might even have surprised me.'

Surprisingly too, she began to enjoy the rest of the evening. Having banished the subject of Danny by some unexpressed mutual agreement, they never seemed to lack for conversation, and when they did lapse into silence it was a comfortable one, the sort of quiet interlude common between friends or people on the same wavelength. Celina smiled at the idea and caught Luke's gaze resting on her, a slightly quizzical expression in his eyes.

'Come and dance,' he suggested as Celina's cheeks began to glow under the close scrutiny.

The club had filled up but there was no difficulty finding space, and after a few moments Celina's self-consciousness vanished and she relaxed, allowing herself to be carried away by the music.

'You're a natural,' Luke complimented her in a lull between records.

'Why, thank you, sir,' she found herself responding playfully. 'You're not bad yourself—considering your age!'

She caught his reaction and laughed, dancing out of range as he seemed about to reach out and hold her, but his mouth was relaxed and she guessed he'd taken her remark in the spirit it was intended, his threat of retribution all part of the game.

But the game took a different turn when the music slowed to a smoochy number. Celina began to walk away, assuming they'd sit this one out, only to be drawn up sharp as Luke's arms came around her shoulder, drawing her back on to the dance area, the touch of his fingers sending currents of electricity pulsing through her.

'Running away?' he asked huskily, pulling her even closer, his arms wrapped around her body, urging her into his, trapping her, exciting her.

She went rigid, shockingly aware of his powerful masculinity, of the havoc he was wreaking on her emotions, but instead of loosening his hold the fingers tightened and Luke dipped his head, resting his cheek against hers.

'Relax,' he whispered softly, his breath a warm flutter on her face. 'I'm not going to hurt you. Relax, Celina, relax.'

And as the music went on without a pause, one slow number after another, she became less rigid in his arms, began to melt against his body, all the time exquisitely aware of the taut muscles rippling against her thighs, those long, long fingers gently stroking the small of her back, Luke's mouth nuzzling her ear, his voice a gentle, hypnotic purr that soothed her senses, filled her veins with deliciously warm sensations. And, just as she found herself wishing, illogically, idiotically, that the night could go on forever, the tone changed and Luke's words brought her down to earth with an almighty crash.

'Marry me, Celina,' he crooned as the haunting strains of the love-song died away. 'Marry me.'

CHAPTER THREE

IT HAD been a nightmare journey home, tense and silent, only Celina's thoughts screaming inside her head. Luke made it all sound so simple, and yet it wasn't.

'You like money?' he had asked, not half an hour earlier, having followed Celina back to their table. 'Of course you do. It opens up a lot of doors. You want money—and yes, Celina, I *know* you do; well, I've got just that——'

'Keep it, Luke,' Celina had interrupted harshly. 'I'm not interested. Not from you.'

'Then you're a bigger fool than I took you for,' had come the sneering reply. 'Why not listen to what I'm suggesting, Celina? It's really very straightforward. I pay you an allowance—a salary if you prefer, a very generous salary—and in return you are to forget Danny and guarantee me two years. At the end of the contract you're a free agent—with a handsome settlement, of course. Interested now?'

'Why me?' she had asked, bewildered. 'You want a wife who's not a wife, yet you could have your pick of women.'

'But I don't want a wife, Celina; that's just my point. Wives make tiresome emotional demands which I've neither the time nor the inclination to pander to. I want a social hostess, someone free from family obligations who can be relied on to organise my personal life, to arrange dinner parties, entertain guests, charm business contacts. As I've said before, I want someone who'll look good at my side, someone I can be proud of. And you're free, Celina, completely independent, which suits

42

me down to the ground. You know the score, you're under no illusions, and I've seen enough of your ability to cope with unexpected setbacks to know that you won't indulge in the tantrums and hysterics that seem the hallmark of so many women. Putting it very, very simply, it's a business arrangement to be terminated as and when necessary.'

'You make me sound so mercenary.'

'Not mercenary, sensible. Look on it as a job, Celina. A fixed-term contract, well-defined, no emotional ties, no recriminations. A two-year contract with an early-termination clause. If you decide to pull out before the time is up, fine, but I'll want three months' notice.'

'No!' Celina had finished her drink in one long gulp before gathering her bag and setting off purposefully in the direction of the cloakroom, neither looking nor caring to see if Luke was right behind her.

'Give me one good reason why not,' he had whispered fiercely, appearing suddenly at her side.

Celina had handed over her ticket, ignoring Luke, or trying to, and wondering impatiently why it should take so long to retrieve one well-worn and not very expensive jacket.

'Are you going to take me home?' she had demanded curtly, ignoring his question as the jacket had arrived and she'd shrugged herself into it. 'Or shall I call myself a taxi?'

Luke's face had darkened, but he'd made no further comment, instead taking hold of her arm, his fingers digging cruelly into her flesh, as he'd escorted her back to the car for the tense journey home.

His words kept ringing in her ears. Why not? Why not? Why not? over and over in time to the sweep of the windscreen-wiper blades, and yet she didn't have an answer, just an instinct, something deep inside that was telling her no. It wouldn't work, not with Luke. Heaven knew, she'd had her doubts with Danny, but marriage to Luke? Celina shook her head. At least with Danny they'd had something in common, would have had fun, would have tried to make it a real marriage. Luke's proposal was something else entirely, something cold and clinical, and yet wasn't that its very appeal?

Celina closed her eyes, too many thoughts battling to be heard. Everything Luke had said was true, but it just hadn't gone far enough. She did need money—oh, not for herself. If only it were that simple.

Her struggle to ease her father's conscience, nurse him back to health, give him back his self-respect, had never seemed more daunting than it did at this moment. And yet Luke was offering a lifeline. Why couldn't she take it, swallow her misgivings, accept his offer of a job? For that was all it was, his strange proposal. And she didn't have an answer. Just pride perhaps, her thoughts homing in on her first reaction, the pain caused by Luke's stinging words, his sneering assumption that money was her motivation, her goal. Money for money's sake.

And supposing she told him the truth, what then? It was nothing to be ashamed of, after all, caring for a sick old man. Only Celina knew how Luke would react. Pity perhaps, scorn, contempt, although he might even be more understanding than the family had been. But he wouldn't want to be involved. No one else had. Family and friends, all the people who'd known her father had disappeared, each and every one of them, like rats deserting a sinking ship. Would Luke be any different? No, he'd feel the same, Celina was sure of it, and then he'd cut the lifeline, withdraw the offer. Her main appeal in Luke's eyes was her apparent isolation. Take that away and he wouldn't be interested. And then she'd be back to square one. Much better not to raise any hopes in the first place; much less cruel not to have to suffer the rejection.

They drew up outside her flat, Celina jumping out before Luke had time to open the passenger-door, her stiletto heels tapping out an angry message. Reaching the front door, she paused, conscious of Luke still beside her, and she spoke without turning. 'Thank you, Luke. I'm all safe and sound now. You needn't waste any more of your valuable time on me. I think I can manage the stairs alone.'

'I'll see you up,' he contradicted with icy politeness. 'And then, Celina, you're on your own. All alone.'

'You know, it might just be the answer that you're looking for,' Anita tossed out unexpectedly, startling Celina.

It was lunchtime and they'd gone shopping, though Celina's role was purely passive. New outfits in this sort of price range never even entered Celina's thoughts, and Anita's favourite boutique was one of London's most exclusive.

'Are you winding me up?' Celina demanded incredulously, catching her eye in the mirror.

Anita continued to twist and turn in front of the glass, critically appraising the cut of the dress, the fall of the skirt, the lines of the bodice. She had been given an account of the evening, a very brief account, Celina skimming over some of the details, still finding it hard to confide in others after years of keeping problems to herself.

'A little too tight, I think,' Anita murmured almost to herself before turning her attention back to Celina. She grinned unrepentantly, ignoring Celina's scowling face. 'It was just a thought, Celina, an idea, a friendly suggestion. You don't have to bite my head off. I was only thinking of you.'

'Hm. With friends like that, who needs enemies?' Celina retorted, but the heat had left her words and her lips were beginning to twitch as she caught the gleam of speculation in her friend's candid eyes.

Anita slipped out of the dress and reached for the next one, a slinky outfit in black and silver that she stepped into, zipped and cursorily viewed before discarding on to the growing pile of rejects that littered the fitting-room floor.

Celina made herself comfortable. If she knew Anita it was going to be a long and probably futile session, with lunch the last thing on her mind. With a bit of luck there'd just be time to grab a coffee and a sandwich before they went back to work, though, if past experience was anything to go on, she wouldn't bank on it.

'It seems a reasonable enough offer to me,' Anita continued, running an eye over the remaining dresses on the rail.

'Oh, sure,' Celina replied, just the tiniest bit sarcastic. 'I put my head on the block, walk into the lion's den, and all you can do is beam approval. Set your heart on a wedding, Anita? Well, you take the plunge. You're not exactly short on offers yourself.'

'Tut, tut,' her friend reproved. 'And you with an English degree, too. Did they teach you nothing about mixing your metaphors at that university of yours?'

'Apparently not,' Celina agreed. 'But the quality or otherwise of my education isn't the subject under discussion.'

'Ah! Giving Luke's offer a little bit of thought now, are we?' Anita trilled gleefully, her grin broadening as Celina flushed under her knowing gaze.

'Not at all,' Celina denied, her colour deepening. 'In any case, it's too late now. The mood Luke was in on Friday when he left me, I'd be lucky if he gave me so much as the time of day.'

'But the question is, would you want him to?' Anita slipped in slyly before turning her attention back to her choice of outfit.

Celina's thoughts drifted. She'd tried not to think of Luke at all over the weekend but the more effort she made, the more he seemed to intrude, his features super-imposing themselves on her mind. She'd thoroughly enjoyed their evening out—the last forty minutes excepted, of course—and had begun to view Luke in another light, and the realisation that they'd buried their animosity and embarked upon a whole new phase in their relationship had taken her by surprise. She smelled danger and, like an animal scenting a trap, she wanted to draw away. It didn't make sense. Why should a man like Luke, young, rich, good-looking, be content with a marriage of convenience? True, he wanted to make sure that she couldn't marry Danny, but he'd managed that already, interfering, arranging, sending Danny away. There *had* to be more to it than that, surely, but, whatever his motives, Celina had no intentions of handing herself to him on a plate.

Her lips twisted wryly. Some hope after Friday. Luke was out of her life now—for good, and it was definitely safer that way. It meant he couldn't wear her down, persuade her to fall in with his suggestions. Celina was only human, and if Danny could catch her on the raw so could Luke. No, she was on her own, and, if that still left the problem of her father, well, she'd cope. She'd managed up till now and it never had been easy. She shivered, though the atmosphere in the dress-shop was oppressive, and then realised that Anita had been speaking, had asked a question, was waiting patiently for Celina's reply.

'I'm sorry,' she admitted, pulling herself together. 'I must have been miles away. What did you say?'

'The frothy red lace or the slinky silver satin. Which do you think?'

'Neither,' Celina told her frankly. 'They're both too brash, too obvious. Have the green taffeta. It's simply perfect for your colouring, and, wearing that, you'll have every unattached male at the party swooning at your feet.'

Anita laughed. 'I'm not sure that I like that idea,' she admitted. 'It's much more fun when they're playing hard to get.' She sighed ruefully. 'But I suppose you're right. You usually are. I'll take the green. What will you be wearing?' she added casually, climbing back into the skirt and blouse she wore to work.

'Me?' Celina was startled. 'I shan't be going, not now.'

'And why not, miss?' Anita demanded. 'Just because that rat Danny Harcourt let you down doesn't mean the rest of the human race have to treat you like a leper. Besides, Mum and Dad are expecting you. Everything's arranged and the seating plan's been finalised. If you drop out now you'll cause chaos as well as disappointing me. Do say you'll come,' she added, changing her tone, coaxing. 'It won't be any fun without you. Please, Celina.'

'And if I say no?' Celina asked, raising a quizzical eyebrow.

'You'll miss all the fun, won't you?' Anita retorted.

'I'll miss you with your string of conquests, you mean. All right,' she conceded with a smile. 'I'll be there. Satisfied?'

Anita nodded. 'You won't regret it,' she told her. 'And that's a promise.'

Celina wasn't too sure about that but she fell in with the suggestions anyway, giving in gracefully when Anita insisted that she had 'just the outfit' for Celina to wear. It wasn't the first time Anita had come to her rescue, happily throwing open her wardrobe for Celina to choose something different for a special night out with Danny.

John Benson, Anita's father, was a well-known figure in the City, his business acumen almost legendary. He was a self-made man, having started out without a penny, but he'd amassed his first million by the age of twenty-three and had never looked back.

Despite this, or because of it perhaps, Anita was fiercely independent, insisting on her own career, her own flat, her own lifestyle, firmly rejecting any offers of help from her family, determined to prove her own worth. Her parents didn't exactly approve but they sat back and allowed her to pursue her own life, insisting in turn that birthdays and Christmas were times of indulgence. Their gifts of money could be invested, they pointed out truthfully. She didn't have to spend it. And Anita, too, hadn't Celina's drains on her resources. She could easily afford the designer-label clothes, exclusive handmade footwear, the expensive little extras that Celina had schooled herself never to yearn for.

But, if life had been easy for the only daughter of one of England's richest men, it hadn't turned her into yet another spoiled rich kid. Anita was one of the most tactful and understanding and generous-hearted of people, and Celina never ceased to be glad that they were friends.

She was ready much too early, beginning to feel nervous and not exactly looking forward to the evening ahead. Silver-wedding celebrations were the last thing Celina felt ready for. She ought to have been going with Danny, but it wasn't his absence that unnerved her. There was something else, something she couldn't put her finger on, a strange intuition that was eating away at her mind.

She went over to the window, raising the blind, staring out into the night. Dusk was beginning to fall, one or two street-lamps glowing amber then orange, the shadows lengthening even as Celina continued to lean her head against the glass.

Anita was sending a car, overruling Celina's alternative of going by taxi, so at least she could fill the waiting minutes in the warmth of her flat.

She moved away, going back to the bedroom, checking her appearance in the full-length mirror attached to the side of the wardrobe. It wasn't entirely successful, the room much too small for Celina to stand far enough back for a decent impression. She frowned. She'd do.

And then she smiled. She'd more than do, thanks to Anita. The dress— 'It simply doesn't suit me, Celina. I can't think why I bought it. I want you to have it, and no buts. It's yours.' —could have been tailor-made for Celina, so perfect was the fit. It was a deep midnight-blue velvet, simplicity itself in style, sleeveless, backless— 'Almost frontless!' Celina had gasped when she'd first set eyes on it, but the bodice hugged her curves, highlighting the generous swell of her breasts without revealing more than modesty would allow, and the swirling calf-length skirt skimmed her hips exactly.

An old pair of strappy white shoes had been successfully dyed to match, and a borrowed shawl completed the outfit. Yes, Celina nodded solemnly at her reflection, she'd do.

The doorbell rang and a shiver of alarm, quickly stifled, ran through her. Now she really was being fanciful. She grabbed her bag, checking its contents for tissues and comb and keys, and, satisfied that she had everything she needed, flung open the front door.

'Hello, Celina,' Luke drawled lazily, his eyes dark and unreadable in the dim light of the hallway.

'You!' she gasped, almost staggering backwards with the shock.

'The very one,' he agreed with faint amusement, sweeping off an imaginary cap and bowing low in mocking subjugation. 'And if madam is ready,' he added easily, 'her carriage awaits.'

She'd recovered much of her composure by the time they arrived at the hotel, the fifteen-minute journey undertaken in silence. Luke had seemed to sense her mood and wisely left her to her thoughts, and Celina had used the time to take half a dozen deep and calming breaths, get herself in hand. She needed her wits about her. It was going to be a long, long evening.

Anita stood with her parents, greeting the arrivals, and Celina shot her a dagger-filled glance as their eyes met. Completely unabashed, Anita grinned wickedly.

'Hello again,' she purred, shaking Luke's hand and glancing provocatively up into his face. 'I'm so glad you could make it. Enjoy yourselves,' she added impishly, her gaze sweeping from Luke to Celina and back again.

'I'll do my best,' Luke replied with gentle irony.

'I'll see *you* later,' was all Celina had time to whisper before the line of people moved on and they were heading for the ballroom.

But by fair means or foul Anita managed to avoid bumping into Celina. When they went in to dine the arrangement of tables made it difficult to converse with anyone other than immediate neighbours, and Anita, as expected, sat with her parents, beaming brightly across the sea of heads whenever Celina's eyes caught hers. As the evening progressed and the music grew louder and the dance-floor became packed with gyrating bodies, the only glimpses Celina caught of her were fleeting ones, Anita smiling flirtatiously at a dance partner in the middle of the floor, or sailing blithely past, a different man in tow each time.

'I wasn't aware that you knew the Bensons,' Celina commented at length, Luke remaining strangely silent on the subject and curiosity getting the better of her.

'We have slight business connections,' he replied, and then, infuriatingly, changed the subject.

Celina bit her lip, itching to know who—or what—had manipulated fate into throwing them together again, but pride not allowing her to pry further. Besides, she didn't need a crystal ball to work out the answer for herself. The coincidence was too outrageous to have occurred by chance. The entire charade shrieked Anita's influence, though why Luke had chosen to fall in with it was another mystery and would, unless she managed to catch Anita alone for a moment, probably remain that way.

Just as she'd resigned herself to the fact that Anita had out-manoeuvred her, Celina caught a fleeting glimpse of green taffeta disappearing through a nearby doorway. She seized her chance. Excusing herself to Luke, she hurried out, halting in the foyer, eyes searching across the sea of heads for some sign of her friend. Unsuccessful at the first attempt, she started again, more slowly this time, a systematic sweep of heads and faces which also drew a blank. It was no good; Anita had been too quick, had vanished, could be anywhere, unless—of course! The powder-room.

'Got you!' Celina murmured, striding quickly across.

It was an L-shaped room with a single exit, and Celina positioned herself near the door. She had Anita cornered; she could afford to be patient. A full five minutes later, hair freshly brushed, lipstick carefully renewed, perfume dabbed on her pulse-spots, Celina was beginning to drum her fingers on the marble-effect surface of the vanity unit. Six or eight women had brushed past on their way out, none of them Anita, and she was rapidly reaching the conclusion that she must have been mistaken. Either it hadn't been Anita she'd spotted in the first place, or, once more, she'd given her the slip.

Annoyed at having wasted so much time, she snapped shut her clutch-bag and swung round, heading for the door when a snatch of conversation from the concealed arm of the L halted her.

'Luke Sinclair,' the woman's voice repeated. 'Of course it is. I'd recognise him anywhere.'

'Then why isn't he here with Maressa?'

'Didn't you hear? Oh, yes! I'd forgotten you've been away.' The voice dropped slightly, confidentially, but still managed to drift clearly across to Celina, rooted to the spot, not wanting to eavesdrop but incapable of tearing herself away. 'Maressa Majors left him high and dry.

An American apparently, fabulously wealthy. Yes! I thought that would surprise you. Surprised Luke, too. He was devastated, really took it badly. He hasn't been seen out twice with the same girl since.'

'But I saw Maressa only last week, coming out of that new boutique in Bruton Place.'

'Oh-ho! Back in town, is she? The divorce must be through, then. Well, well, that's interesting. I wonder how long it will be before she gets her claws back into Luke? Not long, I'll bet.'

The door opened then, swallowing the rest of the conversation in a blast of noise: laughter, the buzz of voices, the melodious strains of the orchestra. Celina started guiltily, aware that she was—unintentionally—being rude, and forced herself to move.

Outside in the foyer, she halted, taking stock, her mind working overtime. She'd known from Danny, of course, that Luke and Maressa had been close, had been expected to marry, but that somewhere along the way something had gone wrong. Danny had been sparing with the details and Celina hadn't pressed him, having had no interest at the time in Luke and his problems. It had all happened before she and Danny had met, and if Luke was broken-hearted he'd covered the fact well, never seeming short of company—young, beautiful female company, needless to say. It was the obvious balm for a wounded ego, Celina now realised, seeing it all from a new perspective, at the same time wondering if Luke was aware of Maressa's return. But no, he couldn't be. With Maressa back in his life he wouldn't be wasting his time on Celina, would he? It was an interesting thought and one that shouldn't really have affected her. Curiously, though, it did.

'Penny for them,' Luke offered half an hour later as they left the dance-floor and regained their seats.

'Sorry?' Celina queried, still deep in thought and not quite following.

'You look as if you're miles away. Finding the company tiresome, Celina? I know I'm second best, but do you have to make it quite so obvious?'

Celina stiffened. 'I didn't ask you to bring me here tonight,' she told him coldly, 'but, if you must know, I was wondering why you did. Guilty conscience, Luke?'

'Not at all. I've done nothing to be ashamed of. But, since we are here, and since we are——' he paused, lips curling in derision '—together, doesn't it make sense to make the best of the situation and actually try to enjoy ourselves? Leastways, that's how I see it. You're entitled to a different viewpoint, of course, so, if you're really hell-bent on being miserable, go ahead, don't let me stop you.'

She flushed, partly in anger, partly in annoyance, aware that she'd over-reacted, that her nerves were somewhat frayed, and vaguely wondering why. She wanted to apologise but pride wouldn't let her, and they lapsed into stony silence, Celina turning her body slightly away from him, her back ramrod straight as she watched other couples seated about the room or shuffling lazily around the dance-floor. Fresh drinks arrived and she reached for her glass, almost draining the contents in one, at the same time managing to convey without speaking that she wanted another. She caught Luke's raised eyebrows and bristled visibly, daring him to comment, but still he didn't speak, merely nodding to the waiter, who returned a few minutes later with two bottles of tonic water and two glasses, one of them empty. The glass with the vodka he placed in front of Celina.

'Aren't you drinking?' she asked, forgetting for the moment that they weren't exactly on speaking terms.

'One of us with a hangover tomorrow is enough,' he replied tersely. 'And if I were you, Celina, I'd make that my last.'

'But you're not me, and you don't own me, Luke, and if you did I'd still have a mind of my own. I'll decide when I've had enough.'

'Inebriates don't make very sober judges,' he retorted.

'I am not drunk.'

'No.' A slight pause. 'Yet.'

'And what's that supposed to mean?' she demanded, eyes shooting flames.

'You've already had two glasses of wine with dinner, Celina. Just take it easy, that's all.'

Celina dropped her gaze. She couldn't be angry. He was right. She was light-headed and she could hardly blame Luke for his concern. And he'd done her a favour in a way. It wasn't the easiest of evenings but it could have been a lot worse, she could see that now. Arriving unescorted, pretending not to care, tactfully fending off the more amorous of dancing partners before slipping off early while no one was looking. They might both be second choices but Celina had gained more than Luke from Anita's meddling, and in that case the least she could do was make an effort.

She took a deep breath. 'Luke,' she began hesitantly, leaving her glass untouched.

'Celina?'

'Look, this is ridiculous.'

'If you say so.'

'Stop baiting me. Can't you see I'm trying to apologise?'

'Apologise? Well now, there's a turn-up for the books,' he sneered, his whole expression ugly. 'What's the matter, Celina? Beginning to wonder if your glass coach is about to turn into a pumpkin? I'm sure you'd survive—after all, it wouldn't be the first time you'd had to cope with such a let-down. But no, it doesn't look too good, does it, men walking out left, right and centre? Bad for the reputation. Bad for the ego too, no doubt.'

'Have you quite finished?' Celina demanded, hanging on to her temper—just. It was on the tip of her tongue to throw his remarks back in his face, to remind him that she wasn't the only one to have been left in the lurch just lately, but that would be dragging herself down to his level and so she bit her tongue, scowling across at him instead.

'Finished?' he queried silkily, pinning her with his gaze. 'Oh, no, Celina, I haven't even finished warming up.'

'In that case, Luke, save it for someone who's listening, since I, for one, am not.'

'The truth hurts, doesn't it, my dear?'

'Your twisted definition of it? No, Luke, sorry to disappoint you,' she retorted sweetly, 'but you don't have that much influence.'

'No?'

'No!'

There was a loaded pause while her words sank in, and Celina tensed, expecting a swift reprisal. Instead, Luke threw back his head and laughed, the unexpected sound triggering a reaction as something at the very heart of her began to melt, began to flow in her veins, began to fill her with a strange, unnerving glow.

'You know, you really are the most provoking woman I've ever encountered,' he observed mildly once his mirth had subsided.

'Oh?' Celina murmured, recognising instinctively the subtle change in atmosphere and wondering why it made her feel uneasy.

'"Oh"! Is that all you have to say? No barrage of questions, no righteous indignation? No hysterical demands for an explanation? You're doing it again. Confounding me. Refusing to live up to my preconceived ideas about the female of the species.'

'Never underestimate a woman,' Celina chided, but her mouth was curving upwards as she relaxed again, easing away the wary expression in her eyes.

'I'll try,' Luke countered lightly. 'But with your gift for surprises, Celina, something tells me I'll be wasting my time.'

'Is that another of your——?'

'Backhanded compliments?' he interrupted with a grin. He added enigmatically, 'Well, if you don't know, Celina, who does?'

By mutual consent they left at midnight, slipping away unnoticed, the journey back to Celina's flat a lot less fraught than their last one. She smiled to herself in the darkness as she compared the two evenings, glad now that they'd patched up their differences, weren't about to part again on bad terms. But the evening wasn't over yet, was it, and would it really be tempting providence, inviting Luke in for coffee? It would be safer not to, but rude in the circumstances, cowardly too. Besides, Luke could always refuse if he wanted to. She'd ask. Luke could decide.

He did. 'Thank you, Celina. Coffee would be lovely.'

Which is how he came to be stretched out on her settee, jacket abandoned, shirt open at the collar, sleeves pushed up above the elbow, the picture of ease, while Celina took the chair opposite, amazed at how natural it felt for him to be there. He seemed in no hurry to be gone, accepting a second cup of coffee despite Celina's warnings that it was only instant.

'That's new,' he observed of the picture above the fireplace. Celina glanced across, surprised that he'd noticed, the only other time he'd been inside her lounge so full of bitter words and temper that she wouldn't have expected him to remember the colour of the carpet, let alone recall the furnishings.

She nodded. 'It's a print,' she explained, omitting to mention that it came out of last week's Sunday supplement and just happened to fit nicely into an old frame. 'Lord Street,' she added almost as an afterthought. 'In Southport.'

'One of the widest shopping streets in England, I believe.' He laughed at her start of surprise, swinging himself up and across, standing in front of it, arms folded across his chest as he craned his neck at the detail. 'The original must be worth looking at.'

'The painting or the street?' Celina enquired, slightly tongue-in-cheek.

Luke grinned. 'Both, I guess. What made you leave?'

The question came as a shock, and Celina choked on her mouthful of coffee. 'You've been ch-checking up on me!' she stammered angrily, the colour flooding her cheeks as she sat bolt upright.

Luke raised an eyebrow. 'For an intelligent woman, Celina, you can be incredibly naïve on occasions.'

'You've no right. How dare you, how dare you delve into my private life? It's—it's—it's——'

'An invasion of privacy?' he supplied in the same mild tone. 'You surely didn't expect me to allow Danny to throw himself away on some little Miss Nobody from heaven only knows where? Of course I checked up on you. It's a very brief dossier. "Born 1966 at Southport, Merseyside. Only child of Sarah, née Monaghan, and Francis Somerville. Mother killed in a car accident in 1977. Father died suddenly in late 1988, shortly before which Celina Maria Somerville had removed herself from the afore-mentioned sedate holiday resort in the northwest and relocated in London. Education: the High School, Birkdale, and Warwick University. Second-class honours in English leading to present occupation: librarian. End of report."'

'So, what would you like to know? The size of my shoes? My blood group? My taste in clothes? Favourite movie-star? Come, Luke, don't be shy.' Celina's voice oozed sarcasm. 'There must be a hundred and one details your sleuth has missed. How often I clean my teeth, wash my hair; my brand of washing-up liquid; the time of the train I caught from Liverpool to London in January 1989; the number of the bus——'

'All right, Celina, I get the message. You can spare me the rest.'

'But no, Luke, it makes such fascinating listening and you must be simply dying to discover all those little things that make me tick. And to think you even contemplated marrying me despite such huge gaps in your knowledge. Why, I could tell you——'

'I'm sure you could, however——'

'So do let me continue,' Celina rushed on. 'You sit back and make yourself comfortable. Shall I fix you another coffee?' She sprang up, reaching for his cup, pausing in the doorway, eyes dancing merrily. 'Now, what shall I tell you next? Oh, yes, I know——'

'Skip it, Celina,' Luke interrupted, but his tone was good-natured enough and Celina chose to ignore him.

'I once played the fairy in the school play,' she told him, moving into the kitchen, her voice echoing as she raised it. 'I must have been all of six. Tinkerbell. Yes, that's the part I played, Tinkerbell. Milk?' she asked, reappearing with the coffee and placing the cups on the table. 'Sugar? Help yourself. Now, let me see. What else would you like to know? Childhood illnesses—the usual ones, I suppose.' She began to tick them off on her fingers. 'Mumps, measles, chicken-pox, glandular fever—that's a nasty one,' she informed him confidentially. 'It nearly blew my A levels; threw the system completely haywire, and then——'

'Woman!'

'Yes, Luke?' Celina was innocently wide-eyed, though the laughter had risen in her throat and the effort of suppressing it was almost choking her.

'I give in.'

'I thought you might,' she answered pertly, allowing her amusement to surface. She regained her seat and they lapsed into silence, a companionable silence.

Surprisingly she did find herself talking about her childhood.

'Mother was a bit of a Tartar, but I could always wrap Dad around my little finger. They never quarrelled, except over me. Mother insisted he spoiled me rotten, Dad always replied that he balanced it out, then, as she was always so strict.'

'And who won?'

'Oh, Mother, of course. She'd clamp her lips together in a thin, disapproving line and carry the air of a burnt martyr around for days. She was right, I suppose; Dad was a soft touch, and not just with me. He couldn't abide to see anyone unhappy and would go to great lengths to make it up to her.'

'She sounds a bit of a tyrant,' Luke observed.

'Yes, I suppose she was. A well-meaning one, at any rate. Still, they were happy enough.'

'Till the accident.'

'Yes.' Silence. Memories swamping back, happy ones, painful ones, unbearable ones. Celina closed her eyes for a moment, seeing her father's face when they brought him the news, hearing once again the awful, racking sobs which he'd tried so hard to stifle, trying to be brave, for Celina's sake. And he'd never fully recovered, and now—— Celina shuddered. Tears forced their way out from underneath her eyelids, sliding down her cheeks. She brushed them away, reaching for her bag, fumbling for a tissue.

'Here, use this.' Luke pressed a folded handkerchief into her fingers. 'Want to talk about it?' he asked a few minutes later. He had left her alone, though he hadn't gone far, returning with a small glass of brandy, almost all that was left of a bottle given as a present the Christmas before and saved for special occasions.

'Thank you. He was a broken man,' she told him when the strong drink had breathed a little warmth back into her. 'He was never the same. Oh, he tried. He tried so hard for me, but he was never the same man. When she died, part of him was buried alongside her.'

'And now he's gone too. It must have been hard for you.'

Celina looked up, startled, something strange having just struck her. Like Danny, Luke assumed that her father was dead, but, unlike Danny, Luke had made enquiries, should have known the truth. But he didn't! Suddenly it seemed so very important that he did. She met his glance. The blue eyes had softened, the look on his face invited confidence. She took a deep breath. She *would* tell him, and perhaps the knowledge would trigger his understanding, would help to moderate his contempt, would show him that she wasn't the money-grabbing bitch he'd taken her for.

'I do know how you feel,' he said before she could begin. 'I lost my father too when I was young. Divorce robbed me of him at six, and then he emigrated. It was worse than death in some ways. At least death is final; you can make a start on rebuilding your life. With this sort of separation you keep on hoping. Each time the phone rang I expected it to be him, telling us he was coming back. Every time the doorbell went I'd hope against hope that he'd be standing there, a crooked grin on his face, a look of hope in his eyes. But it never was.'

'And you never saw him again?' Celina asked, her heart going out to him.

Luke shook his head. 'He remarried, had another family, three half-sisters I never knew. I guess he forgot he had a son. I hated him. For a long time I hated him. And then he died. That was when I found out he had never forgotten.'

Celina raised her eyebrows in gentle enquiry.

'He left me a fortune,' he said simply. 'The girls were well provided for, but the bulk of it came to me.'

'That must have been some consolation,' Celina ventured, not sure what was expected.

'I didn't think so at the time. If anything I was even more bitter. But since then I've had time to think, and mine wasn't exactly a deprived childhood. I still had my mother, a stepfather, a half-brother. Danny made up for a lot. Still, I shouldn't bring him up now, should I?'

Celina felt herself flushing. 'He is your brother, Luke; we can hardly ignore that.'

'No. But mentioning Danny's name to you is like waving a red rag at a bull. Your expression changes and the next thing I know we're up to our ears in a quarrel again.'

'And whose fault is that?' Celina found herself asking, the atmosphere shifting alarmingly.

Luke's eyes narrowed. 'Mine, Celina—apparently. You can't face the fact that Danny might have changed his own mind, can you?'

'I could in other circumstances.'

'Such as?'

'If, for instance, he'd told me himself. It isn't Danny's style, standing me up like that. Danny's too thoughtful, too kind.'

'Too soft, you mean,' Luke snorted.

'Too trusting of big brother,' Celina flashed.

'He'll thank me one day.'

She rounded on him. 'So you admit it was your fault Danny didn't turn up for the wedding?'

'Not at all,' Luke replied smoothly. 'You're putting words into my mouth. I merely meant that once Danny's had time to think about it, he'll realise what a huge mistake it was for both of you.'

'But not for you?' Celina demanded hotly. 'You, of course, know so much more than Danny. You couldn't be making the same mistake with your strange proposal, could you, Luke? No, not Mr Superior himself,' she jeered.

He looked across, his face impassive. 'I keep telling you, Celina, it's a job I'm offering, nothing else. But do have it your own way if it makes you feel happy. It was only an idea, but clearly not a tempting one. If you can afford to be choosy. . .' He shrugged. 'My mistake. Forget I ever mentioned it.'

Celina didn't answer, his words too close to the truth for her denial, and she flushed guiltily under the candid gaze. Dropping her eyes, she stood up, gathering the cups, unconsciously signalling that the evening was over.

Luke retrieved his jacket from the back of a chair, fishing the car keys out of his pocket, and there was an awkward pause while Celina struggled to meet his eyes, struggled to find the words to thank him for an enjoyable evening, for, she had to admit, the time had simply fled and she had enjoyed it once they'd called a truce; up till now, that was.

'Luke——'

'Goodnight, Celina,' he interrupted—wearily, it seemed, crossing to the door as she stood and watched, her emotions in turmoil. 'Good night.'

And as he started down the stairs, his tread heavy on the shabby carpet, some sixth sense told her that this time he wouldn't be back, that this time the goodnight was final, that this time he was walking out of her life— and he was never coming back.

The pain came out of nowhere, slicing through her body, freezing the blood in her veins while pictures flashed unbidden in her mind—her father, broken-hearted, confused, pathetically fragile; her own life starkly empty, meaningless, futile. She acted instinctively, fear jerking her out of her misery, catapulting her out of the door, adding intensity to the single word torn from somewhere deep within her.

'Luke!'

Her voice echoed in the empty hallway, mocking, fading.

The footsteps halted. The silence screamed inside her head. A door banged in the distance, killing the faint hope in her heart, and then Celina heard the sound she was straining to catch, hardly daring to believe, hardly daring to breathe. The footsteps grew louder as Luke retraced his steps. Rounding the corner of the final flight, he stopped, his face impassive under the dim light of the single naked bulb.

'I've changed my mind,' the voice said simply. 'I will marry you if the offer's still open.'

CHAPTER FOUR

SIX twenty-five. Too early even to think of getting up. Celina snapped off the bedside lamp and turned over. Normally after such a restless night she would have got up, made herself a welcome cup of tea, and then climbed back into bed with a book. But this morning, even by the widest stretch of the imagination, could hardly be called normal, and so she burrowed into the pillows, trying to shut off her mind, trying to make up for the hours of lost sleep.

Luke's face had punctuated her dreams, his words haunting her waking hours, and when it hadn't been Luke the other memories had crowded in, jostling for position in a brain already teeming with doubts and uncertainties.

Wearily she thumped the pillow, wriggling herself down into a more comfortable position, determined to close her eyes for another half-hour at least. It was no use. In desperation she started counting sheep. One, two, three, four...ninety-six, ninety-seven...

She woke with a start, conscious that daylight was filtering through the curtains. For a moment she was confused, jolted awake in a strange bed in a strange room. And then she remembered. Her wedding-day. Take two. Her smile was ironic. She supposed it did have a funny side.

If Luke had been surprised at her abrupt change of mind his features had given nothing away. Celina had been the more shocked, both by her own actions and Luke's calm control. He'd barely paused for breath, reeling off a barrage of questions concerning the validity of her passport, the procedure for leave of absence, her preference for a honeymoon, a dozen other details Celina would never have thought of, and, despite the lateness of the hour, spending the next twenty minutes on the phone to the airports.

By the time he'd left less than half an hour later, Celina's head was spinning. Shell-shocked, she had gone to bed, lying awake in the darkness, still not fully believing that in four days' time she would be marrying a man whom she barely knew—or liked. And, if Celina found it hard to take in, Anita, not surprisingly, was speechless.

'You're setting me up,' she had declared once she'd recovered her equilibrium. 'You're paying me back. This is your revenge for Saturday, isn't it?' Her smile had widened in confident assurance that she'd worked it all out. 'Good try, Celina, but I'm not falling for that one hook, line and sinker.'

Celina had smiled enigmatically, refusing to be drawn, merely restating that the wedding was set for eleven o'clock Wednesday, that her request for leave of absence had been granted, and that, since it was Anita's day off, she'd be most obliged if she could act as a witness.

It was Tuesday afternoon before she'd finally admitted that Celina might—just—be telling her the truth, and even then her unbridled delight had alternated with quiet moments when Celina could almost see inside her mind, could almost hear the unspoken questions.

'You seem more jittery than the bride,' Celina had remarked. 'Shouldn't it be me who's suffering from nerves and having second thoughts?'

'You're deadly serious, aren't you?' Anita had asked one last time. 'Oh, heavens, Celina, this will teach me to meddle in other people's lives! Suppose it's a disaster; suppose it doesn't work out? Suppose Luke turns out to be another prize rat? Just think how I'll be feeling.'

'Too late for that,' Celina had countered briskly. 'Besides, at the end of the day it was my decision, not yours. And I hope, I really do hope, that I know what I'm doing.'

But she hadn't been sure, and as she lay gazing at the ceiling in Anita's spare room she still wasn't sure, could hardly believe it herself, was more than half convinced that Anita was right, that it was a hoax—but Luke's hoax, not Celina's. *He* could be playing games with *her*, setting her up, raising her hopes, dangling the bait and then, at the very moment Celina reached out to take it, snatching it laughingly away. And, with Maressa Majors back in circulation, didn't that seem all the more likely?

'Too late for that' kept echoing inside her head, but it wasn't too late, not yet. She still had time to change her mind. Assuming Luke was serious, she had exactly one hundred and forty-nine minutes before she turned her back on one life and embarked upon another. Plenty of time really to call it all off. Her father's face swam before her eyes, his features racked by pain, his fragile presence almost tangible, and then the door swung open and Anita appeared with the breakfast tray.

'Good morning, Celina,' her friend trilled brightly, placing the tray on the bedside table and drawing back the curtains. Sunlight streamed into the room, filling it with a warm golden glow that raised her spirits, pushed away the lingering doubts. No, a little shiver of excitement ran through her. The decision had been made, and rightly or wrongly she wasn't about to take the coward's way out and change her mind.

They touched down at Beauvais at three-fifteen French time. Celina was glad to be back on firm ground. Her irrational fear of flying had thankfully not manifested itself in the forty-minute journey to the outskirts of Paris but, even so, relief poured over her as the plane glided to a halt on the runway.

'Enjoy the flight?' Luke enquired as Celina stretched, smoothing out the material of the ivory silk suit. Everything had happened so quickly that she hadn't even had time to think about buying another outfit. Luckily it had arrived back from the dry cleaners in pristine condition and even now showed hardly a wrinkle.

'Not especially, but at least it was a short one. I must confess I was surprised, though. I half expected you to whisk me away on a private jet.'

'The privileges of the idle rich?' Luke parried. 'I've never really seen the point. The commercial airlines cover everywhere I want to go and, besides, I may not be poverty-stricken but I'm hardly in the same league as the Duke of Westminster or Richard Branson.'

'No, I suppose not.'

'Disappointed?' he queried with a sly smile.

'Not at all.' Celina flushed at the implication. 'You don't exactly live up to your image, do you?'

'Playboy? I might have been once, briefly, but the image has stuck. It's part of my past, the youthful Luke who didn't recognise a shallow way of life.'

'But not any more?'

'No. My father's influence. He must have known what could happen when money's too easily come by. He tied everything up so tightly that I had to work at the beginning. Afterwards, well, I'd got into the habit. I discovered I actually liked work. I still do.'

Luke whisked them through Customs and out to the waiting car, his easy command of French earning him a glance of admiration from Celina, whose knowledge of the subject was limited to stilted guide-book phrases.

'Where are we going?' she asked, for the first time wondering exactly what his plans were.

'We're in the city of lovers, my love. What better way to start a honeymoon than in the centre of romance?'

Celina felt a shiver of apprehension. She frowned. 'I don't understand. I expected a *gîte* or a villa, somewhere in the country.'

'Not Paris by moonlight? Champagne on the Seine? Don't tell me—you've seen it all before and you weren't impressed.'

'No.' Celina shook her head. 'I've never been to Paris. It's somewhere I've always dreamed about.'

'So what's the problem?'

'Nothing—I suppose.' But the little knot of fear refused to go away, kept gnawing away at her insides, and, as the countryside gave way to suburbs and the road signs indicated that they had almost arrived, Celina grew more nervous. What had she done? She must have been mad, completely mad. It was one thing entering into a business arrangement with a man she hardly knew; it was quite another carrying it through without having studied the small print. It was too late now, but she should have made sure that Luke's idea of a marriage of convenience was the same idea as hers.

She checked her watch, wondering how much longer before they arrived, and then realised from the volume of traffic and the style of buildings that they must be nearly there. She swallowed hard, closing her eyes for a moment, mentally composing herself, and then apprehension gave way to curiosity as she found herself craning forwards in her seat, eager to catch a glimpse of the picture-postcard sights she had read and heard so much about.

'You won't see much just now,' Luke's voice cut into her thoughts. 'Though if you're not feeling tired we could go for a stroll before dinner.'

'I'd like that,' Celina answered, mentally dissecting her luggage for something suitable to wear. 'Are we staying long?'

'In Paris?' Luke looked thoughtful. 'A couple of days, a week, two weeks if you like. Long enough to do all the touristy things—see the sights, climb the Eiffel Tower, take a boat-trip down the Seine. Then, when you've had your fill of the city, we'll move on, head south, visit the châteaux perhaps. Any suggestions of your own?'

'Me?' Celina was surprised. 'I think you've covered everything and, in any case, you know Paris, I don't. I would like to wander round the artists' quarter, but apart from that I really don't mind.'

'You haven't mentioned shopping,' Luke observed.

'Shopping? I hate shopping.' Celina shuddered. 'Why on earth should I want to travel three hundred miles to go shopping? Can't I do enough of that in London?'

'Paris is special,' Luke contradicted. 'Fashion houses abound. Every woman wants a Paris wardrobe.'

'Every woman bar one,' Celina countered. 'In my sort of price range there's not a lot to choose between chain stores in London and anywhere else.'

'Now that I don't believe. That outfit for one didn't come ready-made, nor that velvet creation you dazzled everyone with last weekend. They definitely carry the designer label. You can't fool me, Celina; I know quality when I see it.'

Celina sighed. He was right, in a way, but miles out on his assumptions. 'You still think I've been taking Danny's money, don't you, Luke? What can I say to convince you that you're wrong?'

'Am I? I doubt it.' Luke's voice was cold. 'You didn't answer my question, I notice. Something to hide?'

'About my clothes? None of your business.'

'Wrong, Celina. You're my wife now, and I'm interested, very interested.'

'And I'm still an individual,' she informed him as evenly as possible. She didn't want another argument, not yet. 'You may have bought me, Luke, but I'm not a puppet. I live and breathe, have a mind of my own. I retain the right to make my own decisions, keep my own counsel.'

'Wrong again,' Luke contradicted silkily. 'You've accepted the terms of the contract, Celina, *my* contract, and the first instalment is now due. Call it my commission if you'd rather, call it what you like, but I'm entitled to my pound of flesh, surely?'

'Ah, yes,' Celina almost purred, 'but none of the blood, I seem to remember.'

'Meaning?'

'You can't destroy me, Luke. You can take what you are owed, not a drop more, not a drop less.'

'A literary precedent,' Luke acknowledged with a rueful smile. 'I do believe you're right. Round one to you, Celina, and barely a blow exchanged. You're quite a woman, aren't you?' he added. 'Self-possessed, level-headed, ice-cool under fire. And clearly set on stopping me from getting near the truth. Intriguing, most intriguing. I can see I'm going to enjoy pitting my wits against such a skilled performer.'

'I'm not a plaything,' Celina retorted. 'And, with your capacity for digging into my private life, I'm surprised there's anything left for you to wonder at.'

'I'm only human, Celina. All the money in the world doesn't allow me to climb inside your head and see what makes you tick.'

'That must rankle,' she jeered, forgetting her earlier resolution. 'All that money spent dissecting my background and my life. Not money down the drain, surely?'

'No, but there are some things that money can't buy,' he informed her.

'Oh, really? How awful for you. How do you cope?' she asked with heavy sarcasm.

'I get by,' he answered grimly. 'And I'm a fast learner. I use my head, my eyes, my senses. You're hiding something, I'm sure of it. There's too much that doesn't add up, too many contradictions—expensive clothes but a pathetically shabby flat; an ability to spend other people's money—Danny's money—and yet have nothing to show for it. There's something wrong, very wrong, but whatever it is you'll let it slip one day. You think you're clever, but you'll grow complacent, and when that happens I'll be there, waiting to pounce.'

'Like a cat with a mouse, lift a paw and I'm allowed to run away, and then pow! I'm captive again. Or shall you gobble me up, Luke, digest the bits you want, spit out the residue?'

'What a gruesome analogy. But yes, you're right in a way. I will dissect you, and then, when I've found what I'm looking for...' He let the sentence hang, and, beside him on the seat, Celina felt him shrug his shoulders.

And then I'm out on my ears, she silently finished off for him. She could always tell him the truth herself, of course, but the longer she left it, the harder it got. Besides, she wasn't ready to explain—to anyone. Anita had an idea, but even with her friend Celina had been reticent, giving out the sketchiest of pictures. It wasn't shame that kept her silent but pain, the naked hurt of rejection, and not of herself but of her father. He'd been to hell and back, had endured the accusations and shouldered the blame. He'd made a mistake but he'd admitted it, was ready to pay. The shame, the whispers, the pointing fingers, he'd suffered them all—until his own family had turned against him. That coming on top of everything else, he'd cracked.

Celina shuddered, remembering so much, the early weeks of fear and anguish, the long months of pitiful recovery, his still precarious state of health. How could she explain all that to a virtual stranger? Perhaps when they knew each other better...? She shrugged. It *was* a possibility, but she wasn't holding out much hope.

They arrived a few minutes later, the taxi pulling up outside their hotel, superbly located between the Champs-Elysées and the River Seine. It was everything Celina had expected and more: imposing façade, uniformed doorman, luxurious décor; the hotel oozed money in a genteel, understated way.

She got a shock, though, when they stepped out of the lift and into their suite.

'There's only one bedroom!' Celina exclaimed, completely unthinking.

Luke grinned. 'We're on honeymoon, Celina. What did you expect—separate floors?'

She bit her lip, swallowing the rest of her comments. At least there were twin beds, she noticed. It *could* have been worse, though not much, she acknowledged with mocking irony.

She feigned indifference, quickly unpacking the single suitcase and hanging her belongings in one of the enormous wardrobes, and by the time Luke emerged from the bathroom, having changed into trousers and a sweater, she had herself in hand and was even beginning to see the funny side of the situation.

They strolled along the banks of the river, deliberately avoiding the well-known monuments, tacitly leaving those for tomorrow or the next day, and the gentle breeze lifted her hair, stirred some colour into her cheeks, helped banish the shadows, and she returned to the hotel in quite a happy frame of mind.

Changing for dinner wouldn't take long. She knew exactly what she'd be wearing, but, even so, she paused in front of the half-empty rails, nibbling her bottom lip, deep in thought. Luke was right. She did need more clothes. But Paris clothes at Paris prices? She shook her head.

They hadn't discussed money, apart from Luke's wild accusations about Celina's spending Danny's, but she supposed they'd get round to it eventually. They hadn't discussed her job either, and she found herself wondering how Luke would take the news that she intended keeping it. He'd probably be one of those chauvinistic husbands who hated the thought of his wife's going out to work, and could well argue that she had a full-time job already, the one he'd given her, social hostess or whatever fancy name he chose to call it. Another argument, she acknowledged with sinking heart, but pushed the thought away. She'd face that one when the time came. And in the meantime she'd relax, try to enjoy herself.

The sound of running water in the bathroom ceased, and she turned to greet Luke, a smile on her face. 'I'm starving,' she told him, taking the proffered arm with hardly a moment's hesitation.

'Good, so am I. Let's go and eat.'

Being so hungry, they skipped the pre-dinner drinks and headed straight for the dining-room. The tables were well-spaced, the lighting subdued, candles flickering in their glass holders. Around them, conversation continued in typical French fashion with everyone seeming to talk at once, voices rising and falling with emotion.

'The seafood's always worth trying,' Luke suggested as Celina struggled with the menu. There were no concessions to the linguistically illiterate, and she was frantically racking her brain for translations of the one or two words that seemed vaguely familiar.

'Urgh! No, thank you. All those slimy oysters and mounds of shellfish with claws and eyes and other offputting characteristics.'

Luke laughed, tossing back his head, white teeth gleaming in the candle-light. 'Don't you like seafood at all?' he asked, filling her glass with iced water.

'Mm.' Celina nodded. 'Prawns, ready-shelled, preferably in mayonnaise. Or cod and chips. Sorry,' she added as Luke's laugh deepened, 'I'm a bit of a philistine with fish. Somehow they always look too much like their live counterparts.'

'Try the *crudités*,' he suggested. 'Unless you don't like carrots that look like carrots.'

'OK, so I'm potty,' Celina agreed good-naturedly. 'But I'd hate to order something and then discover I don't like it. It's such a waste of money, not to mention insulting to the chef.'

'The chef won't even notice, and as for money that's the least of our problems.'

'To you maybe. I'm not in the habit of throwing it around.'

There was a loaded pause.

'No, you're not, are you? It's another of those little mysteries. You've obviously travelled light, and don't balk at wearing the same outfit two days running. One wonders on what—or on whom—you do spend your money.'

'As I told you earlier, Luke, it's none of your business.' She turned back to the menu, to all intents and purposes closing the subject. Thankfully Luke took the hint, even thawing out sufficiently to provide translations of the unfamiliar dishes.

'You didn't order shellfish,' Celina observed once the waiter had gone.

'I didn't want to spoil your first Parisian meal,' he told her. 'All those offputting eyes and claws and things.'

Celina smiled. 'Thank you. Are you always so considerate to your dining companions?'

'Only to the ones who matter,' Luke replied solemnly.

'Oh!' Celina coloured, and was glad of the subdued lighting. She lapsed into silence, turning her attention back to her meal, keeping her eyes fixed on her plate. She thoroughly enjoyed the food and the occasion, though every now and again a little shiver of apprehension ran through her. She kept reminding herself that it was purely a business arrangement, that despite outward appearances it wasn't a real marriage, and Luke wouldn't be interested in claiming the privileges of a real bridegroom. Or would he?

It was still early when they'd finished eating, and Luke suggested a walk. 'Nothing strenuous,' he assured her. 'Just a ten minute wander to work off some of the calories.'

'It was a lovely meal,' Celina acknowledged, 'and yes, I take your point. I should never have eaten all those profiteroles. It wasn't hunger, just greed.'

'And a bride's indulgence. If you can't spoil yourself on this day, Celina, when can you?'

She didn't answer. It was there again, that *frisson* of unease. 'I'll pop up and fetch my jacket,' she said instead. 'I won't be a moment.'

Back in their bedroom the feeling of vague unease took shape. She had a problem, and, with Luke's bed only a couple of feet away from hers, it was a big problem: a delicate concoction of silk and lace that passed for a nightdress. Celina pulled it out and held it against her, her face flaming in the glass. She couldn't possibly wear it now; there just wasn't enough of it. Sharing a room with Luke was going to be difficult enough without giving the impression of being provocative.

She rummaged through her underwear drawer, hoping for inspiration, but the only thing at all suitable was a full-length petticoat, hardly more substantial than the nightie. Still, it would have to do, and with a towelling robe on top she wouldn't feel too vulnerable. Catching sight of her burning cheeks, she smiled ruefully. 'Who are you kidding?' she briskly addressed her reflection. 'Face the facts, Celina: you're petrified.'

It was a beautifully clear night, a myriad stars twinkling down on them, and Celina banished troubled thoughts. She'd take each moment as it came, she decided, falling into step with Luke. It was a more leisurely wander than their earlier one, Celina's shoes not made for anything too brisk, but Luke seemed not to mind their unhurried pace.

Other couples had the same idea, only they strolled hand in hand, stopping for long, lingering kisses under a moon reflected clearly in the ripples of the water. If she closed her eyes she could be back in London. The river hurried past on its journey to the sea, the traffic zoomed by at breakneck pace, the sound of music and laughter carried on the breeze. Only the voices were different, louder than she was used to, accompanied by gesticulating arms.

It was chillier now, and Celina hugged her jacket to her body. It wasn't a heavy weight, but was more suited to the dress than anything else she'd brought with her.

'Cold?' Luke enquired as they reached yet another bridge and stopped to watch the river.

Celina leaned on the parapet. 'Just a little,' she admitted, breathing in the sweet night air.

'Come on, we'll head back now and I'll fix you a warming drink before we go to bed.'

Before we go to bed. Such innocuous little words really, completely out of proportion to the feeling of dread that engulfed her.

They reversed their steps, Celina's heels echoing on the paving-stones. She was acutely aware of the man at her side, their bodies close but not touching, so near and yet so far. Preoccupied, she didn't notice the cracked paving-stone slightly out of alignment with the rest, didn't notice till she tripped and went sprawling forwards.

Quick as a flash, Luke's arm came out to hold her, steady her, and then another arm drew her close, holding her fast in a comforting embrace. At the first touch of his fingers Celina almost swooned. The blood quickened in her veins, the surge of electricity pulsing through her, setting her on fire, leaving her a tingling, quivering mass of raw emotion. She inhaled the musky scent of his aftershave, breathed in the subtle aroma of his clean, healthy body. Luke's eyes were fastened on hers, sending out an unmistakable message of desire.

With a nervous dart of her tongue she moistened her lips, the gesture unconsciously inviting as her gaze flicked to Luke, her eyes holding his, returning the message she read there, flicking away and back again.

Luke smiled, and Celina felt her heart contract, amazed at her reactions, not stopping to think what she was doing, but simply accepting the moment for what it was—a moment of pure magic.

Luke bent his head and his lips brushed hers, a fleeting caress, barely touching yet searing, igniting, fanning the flames. He drew back slightly, his breath a delicate flutter on her cheek, and then his mouth found hers again, still tentative, still exploring, the tip of his tongue tracing the outline of her lips, filling her with ecstasy. Celina moaned as the pressure increased, the kiss deepening, Luke's mouth more urgently demanding, his tongue entwining with hers as the fireworks exploded in her head. It was wonderful, sheer magic, and she never, ever wanted it to end.

And, when at last he drew away, Luke's arms continued to hold her, his hands caressing and stroking as Celina nestled happily into his body, rested her head on his shoulder, was happier than she'd ever been before. The rapid beat of his heart pulsed against her cheek and she smiled to herself. He hadn't been indifferent then; she had the power to stir him.

'Celina, Celina, Celina,' he whispered, his mouth warm against her ear. 'What have we done, my love?' he asked. 'What have we done?'

As the words sank in Celina stiffened. He regretted it, then, so soon; the kiss, the wedding, the entire charade. But his fingers continued to hold her, refused to allow her to pull away.

'Relax, sweetheart,' his voice entreated, soothing, crooning. 'Relax.'

And Celina did, leaning against his powerful body as his hands stroked the small of her back. The minutes ticked by and gradually her breathing quietened, her nerves steadied, her eyes closed as she allowed herself the luxury of enjoying his body against hers.

They strolled slowly back, hand in hand, just another couple in love and in Paris, and for a few precious moments Celina let herself believe it, pushed the stark reality away.

Swallowing her apprehension, she forced herself out of the bathroom. Not even she could justify a single extra stroke of the hairbrush, another thirty seconds spent scrubbing teeth that were antiseptic-clean before she'd even started.

She looked ridiculous and Celina knew it, white towelling robe tightly belted, arms folded protectively across her chest. She willed herself to relax, to look him in the eye, to lower her arms to a more normal position, but she couldn't do it.

Luke didn't speak; he didn't need to. Celina was acutely aware that he was sitting up in bed, propped up against the pillows, arms behind his head, completely at ease. She hadn't even glanced in his direction and yet she knew instinctively that his chest was bare, that the still-tanned body gleamed under the soft glow of the bedside lamp.

'Come here, Celina.' Luke's voice was husky.

Carefully avoiding his eyes, Celina moved in the direction of his bed. An arm reached out, taking hold of her wrist, tugging her gently nearer.

'Sit down,' he commanded, and, 'Look at me, Celina, look at me.'

Slowly she raised her eyes, taking in the powerful build of his body, the shock of hair across the broad expanse of chest, golden and inviting; the determined chin; the smoky depths of his dark-fringed eyes. Such incredible lashes, she found herself thinking inconsequentially, dark and curly, adding intensity to his gaze.

Luke's hands slid up her arms, cupping her elbows, urging her nearer and nearer, but Celina froze, went rigid at his touch, frightened eyes reflecting all her inner turmoil. Luke smiled reassuringly, hands moving up to her shoulders, their very movement a light and delicate caress, and he moved forwards, slowly, infinitely slowly, his face closer and closer to hers until they were almost touching.

'I want you,' he whispered urgently. 'All night I've wanted you.' His lips moved across her cheek, dropping feather-light kisses, moved on, hovered tantalisingly about her mouth and moved down to her throat, each point of contact sending darts of pleasure pulsing through her body. And, while his mouth explored her throat, her neck, her mouth again, his hands and fingers caressed and stroked, tugging her closer, pushing away the robe, which dropped from her shoulders, before deftly disposing of the shoe-string straps of her slip. His mouth moved down, nuzzling, nibbling, and down again, nudging aside the silky material, releasing her breasts from their flimsy restraints, exposing their creamy, blue-veined ripeness to his gaze. He paused for a moment, eyes drinking their fill, his mouth curving into a sensuous, satisfied smile, and then he dropped his head, his mouth fastening greedily on one pink-tipped bud and then the other, sucking, gently nibbling, teasing, lifting her to fever-pitch.

They moved as one, Celina stretched out along the length of the bed, Luke's body bearing down on hers, the contact of his bare chest on her exposed breasts another electrifying sensation, one that sent the blood pounding in her ears, intensified the bitter-sweet agony of the ache inside her womb.

'I want you,' he whispered once more, breath warm on her cheek.

I want you, I want you, I want you, Celina could have sung, but his mouth had claimed hers again and she parted her lips, taking his tongue into her mouth, sucking hungrily, entwining it with hers.

Luke's hands moved lower, following the curve of waist and hip, triggering wave after wave of emotion as Celina surrendered to the magic of his touch. I want you, I want you, I want you, she sang again inside her head, her body moving against his, rising to meet his hands, her trembling response so natural, so right, so wonderful that nothing else mattered, just this man and the touch of his fingers, the brush of his lips, the weight of his body bearing down on hers.

And then she sobered.

He didn't love her. He wanted her; oh, yes, he wanted her. Wanted to take her away from Danny for some twisted motive of his own, wanted to stamp his body on hers, branding her his property, wanted to humiliate, ultimately to discard.

But this hadn't been part of the bargain. She froze, and the probing fingers halted.

For a long, awful moment their eyes locked, Celina's cloudy, silently pleading, Luke's smoky, sultry, the passion dissolving as surprise gave way to dawning comprehension.

'You bitch!' he snarled, his mouth twisting into an ugly, angry line as Celina flinched visibly away from him. He released her, striding forcibly across to the bathroom, and she was left in a heap on the bed, Luke's bed, half-naked, humiliated, unfulfilled. Tears stung her eyes and she let them hover for a moment, wallowing in self-pity. It could have been so, so easy, and yes, she *had* wanted him, but in the cold light of day she would have despised herself, would never have forgiven herself.

The sound of running water in the bathroom told her Luke was showering, and she picked herself up, adjusted the straps of the absurd makeshift nightdress, straightened the sheets still warm from his body and moved woodenly into the sitting-room, where she raided the mini-bar for a brandy. She carried the drink back to her bed and climbed in, pulling the duvet up and around, cocooning herself in an effort to quell the raging, conflicting emotion inside her mind and body.

By the time Luke reappeared, she was halfway down the brandy, felt more in control, though the dull ache of unconsummated passion refused to disappear.

He too, went through to the sitting-room. Celina thought for one heart-stopping moment that he intended sleeping on the sofa, but he returned a few minutes later with a glass and the bottle of brandy.

'I hadn't taken you for a tease,' he said scathingly, voice oozing contempt. 'I knew you were a lot of things— mercenary, ruthless, utterly selfish—but I hadn't reckoned on this. Poor Danny must have had his work cut out.'

'Why drag Danny in?' Celina answered bleakly.

Luke poured himself a drink, moving across to his bed, sitting on it instead of in it, and when he spoke his voice was arctic. 'Isn't Danny the reason for this display of mock-maidenly virtue?' He gave an angry snort. 'I'm the fool. I should have expected it, yet another of your little surprises. Good in bed, was he?'

'Mind your own business!' Celina spat, controlling the urge to spring up and confront him, to wipe the sneer off his handsome face.

'I'm surprised you didn't go through with it,' he jeered. 'You could have made a real comparison then, couldn't you, Celina? Marks out of ten for artistic performance and content. You wouldn't have found me lacking, I promise you.'

'I wouldn't be too sure of that,' she found herself goading. 'Danny's a hard act to follow.'

'So, the truth's out, is it? You're a cold bitch,' he hissed, eyes twin pools of venom. 'Cold and calculating, but you're a fool as well. You're still vulnerable, Celina. Tomorrow I could end this parody of a marriage and then you're back to square one. Penniless. One stroke of the pen and it's all over. Finished. Annulled. Non-consummation's as good a plea as any.'

'And how would that look in the London papers?' she couldn't resist needling. '"City Playboy's Bedroom Technique Found Lacking" sounds sufficiently revealing, don't you think?'

'You'd never make it stick,' he growled, 'any more than I'd be fool enough to try it. In any case, you wouldn't pass the medical.'

'I beg your pardon?'

'For non-consummation. You wouldn't qualify,' he sneered. 'You need to be a virgin. Now, there's a quandary. Talk your way out of that one, Celina, if you can.'

Celina flushed. 'You really are loathsome,' she informed him icily. 'Crawl back under your stone, Luke, and take your cheap and nasty comments with you.'

'And neglect my eager little bride?' he taunted. 'Oh, no, my love, I couldn't do that. We've tied the knot now. We belong together, for the time being, at least. But you needn't worry,' he added, contempt punctuating each and every word. 'There won't be any repeat performances of tonight's fiasco. I like my women willing, and, believe me, there's no shortage of volunteers. You can go your way, and I will go mine. But do me a favour, won't you? Be discreet. "Brother Cited As Co-Respondent" doesn't make pretty reading either.'

'You wouldn't dare!' Celina gasped, dismayed at the nightmare ending to the fairy-tale day.

Luke drained his glass before climbing under the duvet and snapping off his bedside lamp in another gesture of dismissal. 'And that, Celina, is another of your mistakes,' he drawled. 'It's simply not your day, is it, my dear?'

CHAPTER FIVE

CELINA didn't sleep. How could she? There were far too many thoughts screaming inside her head, clamouring for attention. The wedding had been a mistake, the whole idea preposterous. She should never have allowed herself to be persuaded by Luke's easy words. A cold-blooded business arrangement? How naïve, she jeered, how pathetically naïve. It would never work; hadn't they proved that already? Why, they hadn't even cleared the first hurdle.

She lay awake in the darkness, listening to the rhythmic rise and fall of his breathing, her mind reliving over and over again the entire sorry scene: the romantic walk in the moonlight; Luke's lips on hers, demanding, exciting; his hands on her naked body; making love. Love! What a mockery of love their marriage was turning out to be.

Luke despised her—that much was plain. And why not? He had every right to think the worst of her; after all, she'd sold herself, and sold herself cheap. What else was he to think? It didn't help that he was wrong, that he'd misjudged her. It didn't stop the angry words ringing in her ears, tormenting, lashing, punishing.

She turned her head, seeing Luke's tousled head in the half-light, his face unexpectedly vulnerable in repose. She felt a tug at her heart, felt the tears begin to sting, and she closed her eyes, squeezing her lids tightly together, not wanting to watch him, not wanting to remember. But, of course, she couldn't forget. Luke's sneering contempt was stamped indelibly on her mind.

And what if she told him the truth? What then? Would Luke be interested? Would he care about her reasons? Most likely not, she acknowledged miserably. It all sounded so easy in theory but it wouldn't look good, would it, finally admitting among other things that yes, she had taken Danny's money? It wasn't a large amount by any means, and Celina had been desperate, at her wits' end, had accepted the money reluctantly and on her own insistence that it must be regarded as a short-term loan, despite Danny's protestations to the contrary. And the money had never been repaid—not for want of trying on Celina's part, but would Luke understand? No.

Wearily she climbed out of bed, tiptoeing into the bathroom, running herself a hot, scented bath, soaking away her misery. Luke was awake when she opened the bedroom door, propped up against the pillows in painful parody of the night before.

'Good morning, Celina. I hope you slept well. I certainly did.'

'Thank you, Luke,' she replied, taking her cue from him. 'Like a lamb.'

He smiled, but the warmth didn't reach his eyes. 'I'll shower and dress and then we'll go down for breakfast. Give me ten minutes.'

Celina tugged a hairbrush through her hair, watching her reflection, a tiny frown creasing her brow. So that's how he wants to play it, she mused as the tangles of hair were restored to semblance of order. Fine, Luke, we'll play it your way. It doesn't matter, it doesn't even hurt much, and it's easier this way, easier to keep my distance, easier to cope. At least that's what she told herself.

It didn't seem quite that way, avoiding his gaze over breakfast. To anyone watching it was a common Parisian scene, young lovers sharing the sweet hot rolls and butter with tiny cups of strong hot coffee. Only Celina knew

different, her face aching from the effort of holding back
the tears.

'What would you like to do first?' Luke enquired
casually as they finished eating. 'The Eiffel Tower?
Notre-Dame? Sacré-Coeur? Or the salons of *haute
couture*?'

'I told you yesterday I wasn't particularly interested
in shopping,' Celina replied, equally evenly. 'Although
there are one or two things I do need to pick up, but
not in any of the fashion houses, I hasten to add. Oh!'
She broke off, a sudden thought occurring, a tiny frown
of annoyance flashing across her face. Just as quickly
she banished it, presenting an untroubled mien to his
interested gaze.

'A problem?' he asked. 'Something you've forgotten
perhaps?'

'No. That is, nothing important, nothing I can't
handle,' she replied, quickly running her mind over a
list of possibilities.

Everything had happened so quickly that Celina had
overlooked the question of currency. She had English
money with her, but not a great deal, not enough to
carry her through the next two weeks, and, since she'd
been forced to write a hefty cheque for the nursing home
only last week, her bank balance was sadly depleted.

And yet how ironic. Her lips twisted into a bitter smile.
Here she was, on holiday with one of the richest men
in London, and she had barely a penny to her name.
The subject of money had to come up sooner or later,
assuming Luke intended going on with their bizarre arrangement, but in the meantime how was she to get by
without appealing to Luke and giving him yet another
opportunity of branding her a gold-digger?

Celina's heart sank. She hadn't much choice. She'd
change her English notes and cash as big a cheque as
possible, and, when that ran out, well, she'd just have
to swallow her pride, wouldn't she?

They returned to their suite and Celina disappeared into the bedroom to change into ski-pants and a sweater and sensible flat shoes. When she emerged Luke, too, had changed, the faded denims fitting like a second skin, allowing her eyes to trace the firm outline of his powerful thighs. An open-necked shirt and denim jacket completed the outfit, making him seem somehow younger than his thirty-five years.

Needles of pain ran through her again. If only—— She swallowed the thought. A phrase from her childhood sprang to mind, something her grandmother had used to chant for her when she was little. 'If ifs and ands were pots and pans, there'd be no need for tinkers,' she would sing, and Celina would join in, proud that she could remember the words of a ditty that made no sense at all—then. She understood now, though, only too well.

'Ready?' Luke asked.

Celina nodded.

'Good. The Eiffel Tower, I think. We'll take a taxi. It isn't far and taxis are as much a way of life here as they are in London. After that, well, you can choose. After all, it is your honeymoon.'

'But not yours?' she asked, despite her intention to avoid controversial issues.

Luke's expression was grim. 'Apparently not.'

Celina was overwhelmed. Firmly fixed in her mind was the English equivalent of this enormous construction, but the Blackpool Tower, she now realised, wasn't even a poor relation.

'My goodness, it's so big!' she couldn't help saying as they emerged from their taxi and stood, necks craned skywards, looking up at the intricate arrangement of ironwork. 'I didn't expect anything like this.'

'Impressed?' Luke asked, an indulgent smile on his face as he watched her reaction.

'Impressed? I'll say impressed. It's . . . it's . . . it's . . .'

'Awesome?' he supplied. 'I thought that's how you'd feel. It did the same to me, too, the first time I saw it, and even now, several visits later, it still has the power to stir me. Come on,' he took her elbow to guide her through the traffic, 'let's go over.'

Standing at the base of one of the gigantic feet, Celina felt even more insignificant. 'It must be how the Lilliputians felt when Gulliver went visiting,' she confided.

Luke's smile widened. 'Exactly,' he agreed. 'I couldn't have put it better myself.'

Celina watched the yellow lift disappearing into the distance.

'Want to go up?' he asked.

'Can we? Oh, yes, please, Luke. I might never get the chance again.'

He threw her a strange, solemn glance. 'Oh, but you will, Celina; I promise that you will,' he said, and the quiet intensity of the words triggered a thrill of excitement, brought the rush of colour to her cheeks.

Celina was like a five-year-old out on her first expedition. She pressed her face against the glass, devouring the view, totally unaware of Luke behind her, the mixture of languages and accents that surrounded her. Her heart soared. As they climbed higher so did her spirits, picking themselves up from rock-bottom. Whatever else was wrong, this was all too wonderful, and she would remember every tiny detail, impressing it on her mind, would forget the arguments and niggles, Luke's stinging words, would remember only the good parts, would keep in her heart the moments worth savouring.

They went up to the highest level and as they stepped out she gasped. They were safely enclosed but, even so, she felt incredibly vulnerable, only inches away from the thousand-feet drop.

'You can see for miles on a clear day,' Luke informed her, cupping her elbow as they moved round.

Celina found herself welcoming the touch of his fingers. It might not mean a great deal to Luke, but in her eyes it meant they weren't entirely strangers. She didn't know why but she needed him to care, and, if this helped with the pretence, well, it was a harmless enough deception, surely?

Luke pointed out some of the more recognisable landmarks as they followed other tourists around the four sides of the tower. Celina loved it. She thought she could never tire of such a magnificent view and had to stifle a twinge of disappointment when they took the lift down to the first platform.

There was less here than she'd expected, the souvenir shops surprisingly ordinary with their model Eiffel Towers and selection of inexpensive keepsakes, and Celina gave them only the most cursory of glances before halting at a stand of postcards and running her fingers along an assortment of panoramas. She'd send one to her father, she decided, choosing a floodlit picture of Notre-Dame by night. He'd had an interest in church architecture once, a long time ago now, it seemed. Then she remembered. She hadn't any money. She made to replace it.

'Shall I buy it?' Luke asked, seeing her hesitation. 'I don't suppose you've any loose change.'

Celina nodded, grateful for his understanding, and she waited patiently while he popped into the shop.

'I got you a stamp as well,' he told her, handing over the small packet.

Celina slipped it into her pocket. She would write it later, in privacy, and post it in the morning. Her father might not even glance at it but that didn't matter. Make everything as normal as possible, the doctors had told her. Something might just tip the balance in the right direction, start him off on the road to full recovery. It seemed a futile hope at times, but Celina would never give up. She could never live with herself if she did.

She wondered again where Luke had obtained his information. He must have spent a great deal of money investigating her lifestyle, her background, her past, and yet there was this glaring inaccuracy about her father. Whoever had done the research hadn't done a very thorough job. Celina half smiled. Luke would be furious if he ever found out he'd been misled, and not just by Celina. Still, that wasn't her problem. An involuntary shiver ran down her spine. It might not be her problem yet, but she could well imagine Luke's reactions, and it didn't make a very pretty picture.

As if by tacit agreement they wandered down the broad and noisy boulevard. She was more aware of the differences between London and Paris in daylight, the traffic in particular rushing past at breakneck speed, the blaring horns loud testimony to the French drivers' impatience of other drivers and intolerance of pedestrians.

'You take your life in your hands crossing in official places,' Luke informed her, and Celina could well believe it. People gathered on the kerb, one eye on the sequence of lights, one eye on the speeding traffic, and they moved off in a uniform surge that, even so, managed to provoke the screech of brakes, the raised voices of angry motorists.

Celina was more than happy to cling to Luke's arm, not realising that they were halfway down another street and her hand was still firmly anchored to his.

They reached a row of shops, expensive shops, judging from the quality of goods and the absence of price tickets, and Celina halted, her fancy taken by an exotic display.

'Want to go in?' Luke asked as she made to move away.

'Oh, no!' she exclaimed. 'I'm more than happy just looking. It's not often I have the time to stand and daydream. Besides, it's much more fun planning how to spend the money you haven't got on expensive and useless little trifles you can't imagine ever needing than actually shelling out a small fortune for a tiny bottle of perfume that has to last from one Christmas Day to the next.'

'Is that how it is?' he asked in a strange voice.

Celina turned to face him. She sobered at once, her pleasure evaporating under his steady gaze. 'I'm not touting for sympathy, Luke,' she told him firmly. 'Some of us live in the real world, that's all. I wasn't brought up to expect everything I wanted handed to me on a silver salver. Just as well, I suppose,' she added without bitterness. 'If I see something I like then I'll buy it.'

Luke shrugged, holding her gaze for a long moment, his expression unreadable, and then he moved away a little, giving her space.

Celina continued to gaze into the glass, though this time she wasn't seeing the shelf upon shelf of perfume, the row upon row of exquisite jewels. After a few minutes she glanced across at him. He had his back to a window, was still watching her intently. Their eyes met, locked, and Celina stood perfectly still, feeling the colour flood her cheeks, incapable of tearing her gaze away. A message flowed out and across the space between them, was received, acknowledged, returned. For a fleeting moment she was so sure of the signal Luke was transmitting that her heart leapt, her body tingled. She half took a step towards him, expecting him to open his arms, expecting his smile, expecting—she wasn't quite sure what, but it was something wonderful, something right, something natural. Yet, even as she moved, the image shattered, dissolved, and the shutters came down over his face, locking her out. She halted, confused, unable to comprehend her own turbulent emotions, unable to comprehend Luke.

They walked on, side by side, unspeaking, and Celina was glad, not sure she could indulge in small talk until she had herself in hand.

'Fancy a coffee?' Luke asked at long last. 'Or something stronger if you'd rather. It is nearly midday and, as we're in France, why not do as the French do?'

'Thank you,' she replied, and, though sorely tempted to ask for a nerve-soothing brandy, opted for coffee.

They stopped at a pavement café. 'Inside or out?' Luke asked. 'It's not very warm, but the atmosphere's better on the street. You can watch the world go by.'

'Then we'll watch the world go by,' she told him almost brightly as the waiter appeared.

'Do you mind if I leave you for five minutes?' Luke asked once they'd ordered. 'There's something I must do.'

Celina smiled. 'No, you go ahead. I'll be fine.'

The waiter returned, strong, piping-hot coffee for Celina, a small carafe of white wine for Luke. She remembered the postcard. She wrote a simple message and addressed it to the nursing home, putting it back in the paper bag. Luke returned as she was slipping it inside.

'Have you written it? I'll post it if you like. There's a post office on the corner.'

Celina coloured. She shook her head. 'No, I haven't finished,' she lied, acutely aware that Luke knew it too.

His face hardened. 'He won't be interested, Celina,' he remarked icily, pouring his drink.

'It isn't for Danny,' she retorted, tossing her hair back over her shoulder.

'No?'

'No!'

Luke's expression told her plainly that he didn't believe her but he let the subject drop and they lapsed into an uneasy silence. She wondered how much more of this her nerves would take. Nothing she did seemed right to Luke, and tears of frustration were pricking at her eyes again. She didn't like deceiving him, she realised, unconsciously seeking his approval, his approbation. And yet it wasn't all her fault, surely? Luke must take some of the blame. He didn't exactly invite confidence, did he, jumping to conclusions, condemning her out of hand? She sighed, half under her breath. She couldn't blame Luke. He didn't know the truth, and until he did she'd no right to judge his reactions. She'd just have to live with the situation, however uneasy that left her, because at the end of the day she simply wasn't ready to explain.

He slid an envelope across the table. 'I thought you might need this,' he told her as she raised her eyebrows.

Tentatively she picked it up. It was unsealed and she could see without opening it that it contained money, a great deal of money, French money.

'Oh, no, I can't,' she protested, her face flaming. She made to pass it back.

Luke's hand came down on hers, halting her, reminding her of the effect he was beginning to have on her senses. 'Oh, yes, you can,' he told her firmly, but with some indefinable quality in his tone. 'You'll need money, and until we get back to London and sort things out properly I don't want you feeling you have to beg for every penny like a child asking for pocket money. It isn't charity, Celina, it's yours; you've earned it, or you soon will have.'

Celina was choked. He was a man of many facets, she was beginning to discover, a man of hidden depths, one moment coldly ruthless, the next surprisingly thoughtful.

'Put it away, Celina,' he commanded in the same strange voice. 'And one more thing.'

'Yes, Luke?' She swallowed hard.

'You are to spend it, understand? I want you to spend it—on yourself. Blow the lot. Because when that's gone there's plenty more. Understand?'

'Yes, Luke.' And, in a way, she did.

They went on to Les Invalides, Celina having read about Napoleon's tomb, and, though the domed building itself was very impressive, she thought the dark red marble of the tomb hideous and oppressive. The rest of the building housed the museum, more Napoleonic memorabilia, including a particularly gruesome exhibit, in Celina's eyes; Napoleon's dog, which had been stuffed and preserved.

They didn't linger long, hunger-pangs reminding them both that it was lunchtime.

'What would you like to do next?' Luke asked once they'd eaten.

'It's your turn to choose,' Celina told him with a smile.

'In that case, madam, I have just the thing in mind.'

Celina wasn't too sure she agreed once she realised that Luke's plans for the afternoon consisted of wandering around shops, and highly expensive shops at that. She was wary at first, suspecting him of deliberately setting a trap, of tantalising her with a vast array of beautiful clothes and accessories, and then standing to one side while she obligingly proved one of his earlier assumptions.

Gradually, however, she began to relax, deciding she was mistaken. Luke wasn't expecting her to spend, spend, spend for spending's sake, and, once she'd put aside those reservations, she actually began to enjoy the experience.

She was amazed, too. She hadn't realised such shops existed. For so long now she had been on a rigid budget, self-imposed but essential none the less, and had avoided like the plague the sort of shops where a single outfit could cost anything from a month's salary upwards. Her wedding outfit had been the one exception, and that had only been possible after weeks and weeks of scrimping and saving, of existing on a diet of vegetables and wholemeal bread, of walking wherever possible to save on bus and tube fares. Still, she had thought it worth it at the time.

Now, at another time, another place, her head was soon spinning from the dazzling displays of exotic fabrics: tussore silks and watered silks; cashmeres and mohairs; rich deep velvets; gossamer-fine laces; ostrich and maribou feathers; a myriad textures in every shade and hue from the most delicate of pastels to the deepest, darkest midnight colours of blue and black and purple.

Luke whisked her through whole departments of lingerie, separates, accessories, day-wear, evening-wear, furs and frills and 'essential' little fripperies she couldn't believe anyone would ever pay money for, let alone need.

Best of all, though, she loved the boutiques on the Avenue Montaigne, and for the first time began to re-alise that it wasn't just another time, another place, but another world altogether, a world she wasn't sure she'd want to give up once she became a part of it.

'I've a little shopping of my own to do,' Luke told her finally. 'I've deliberately left this one till last because I've a sneaking suspicion that even you won't be able to resist some of these. Laroche was famous for his ability to dress women, instead of disguising them. You won't find anything outrageous here, just beautifully cut, extremely elegant clothes which carry the stamp of a master, and which, with your figure and looks, should make you the envy of women throughout the world. Now there's a compliment for you,' he added with a twinkle as Celina blushed to the roots of her hair. 'Speechless?' he teased as he made an elaborate charade of bending and kissing her hand in a farewell gesture. 'I'll be about an hour and a half. Have fun.'

And have fun she did, completely shedding her in-hibitions, amazed that the hands of the clock moved round to five o'clock so swiftly. The time simply hadn't been long enough to do the boutique justice, for, as Luke had correctly forecast, the ready-to-wear designer clothes had tremendous appeal and, even to someone of Celina's thrifty nature, the classic lines and hallmark of quality couldn't be denied.

Luke smiled his approval when Celina indicated the boxes and packets that comprised her selection, and their short walk back to the hotel was undertaken in chatty description of some of the outfits she hadn't decided to buy.

'I think I'd be more interested in what you did buy,' Luke said when Celina paused for breath.

'Oh, but that would spoil the surprise,' she told him. 'You'll just have to wait and see, won't you?'

She wondered if his own shopping expedition had been equally successful. He seemed satisfied, but there were no tell-tale packages or carrier-bags, and it did cross her mind that it might just have been tact on Luke's part, giving her time to herself, preventing any possible embarrassment as Celina spent money which, despite his protestations, she still didn't regard as her own. It was a nice thought, and served to underline how little she knew about him. But she was learning fast, and, the more she saw of him, the more she liked—a dangerous situation, given the state of their relationship. A pity really. It took the shine off the afternoon.

'Close your eyes,' she commanded, her head the only part of her visible as she prepared to stage her 'grand entrance' into their sitting-room.

Luke obligingly did as he was told, and Celina tiptoed out of the bedroom, double-checking her appearance in the full-length mirror before halting in front of him.

'OK,' she told him. 'You can look now.'

Luke opened his eyes, his face registering a momentary surprise before the genuine smile spread across his features. He gave a low wolf-whistle as Celina pirouetted.

The figure-hugging 'little black dress' fitted like a glove. It was starkly simple, black lace lined with silk, shoulderless, daringly cut at the front, emphasising the upward sweep of her full breasts. It skimmed her waist and hips, followed the contours of her thighs, and ended a demure inch and a half above her knees.

'And where, my lady, are we going tonight?' he asked, his appreciative glance warming Celina's already pink cheeks.

'Why, sir, that is up to you,' she replied pertly, unconsciously flirtatious.

Luke's eyes narrowed. 'With you dressed like that, I think I'd rather keep you here,' he told her, and she couldn't mistake the meaning behind the lightly spoken words.

The pleasure drained away from her face.

'I know. That wasn't part of the bargain.' Luke's voice was bleak. 'But hell, Celina, you can't blame a man for trying. I'm only human, and dressed like that . . . Come on, I think we'd better go out before I say something we'll both regret.'

Celina moved woodenly back into the bedroom. She removed the matching bolero jacket from its hanger, slipping it over her shoulders before going back in to face him, her thoughts in turmoil. She began to realise that their mockery of a marriage wasn't exactly fair on Luke. She tightened her lips. It wasn't fair on her either, she countered in her mind, and then her innate sense of justice rose to the surface. She had known what she was doing. It had been a cold-blooded decision, and yet with Danny it wouldn't have sounded quite so mercenary. And with Danny she had expected a real marriage, a marriage in every sense of the word.

The complication now was that her feelings were becoming involved. She was being drawn to Luke, couldn't bear the thought of hurting him, and, though he never would care for her, not in the real sense, not like a lover, it didn't mean she couldn't try to make him happy, in some ways at least.

'Luke,' she began hesitantly, struggling to meet his gaze, 'I know you had your own reasons for marrying me, and I know we made a bargain of sorts, but that doesn't mean we can't——'

'Don't, Celina,' he interrupted harshly. 'I know what you're saying and, believe me, it isn't necessary; it isn't necessary at all. Forget the whole idea. Now, if you're ready?'

She nodded miserably, half relieved, half disappointed, gulping back the tears. It was going to be another long evening.

Luke had booked a boat-trip, which should have been fun but the early part of the evening was overshadowed by the shaky start. Conversation was desultory and stilted, Luke pointing out landmarks, Celina making suitable noises of acknowledgement.

'It's very beautiful,' she told him at last, making a huge effort to be enthusiastic. Every bridge, every major building, fountains, squares, monuments, all were bathed in light, the reflections in the fountains and river creating the effect of a fairy-tale city. 'Beats Blackpool every time,' she added, attempting to lighten the atmosphere.

'I've never been,' Luke confessed, following her lead. 'Living in London, we tended to go to Brighton for the day and somewhere abroad for our holidays. I always envied kids who lived in seaside resorts. You don't know how lucky you were growing up in Southport.'

'It has its good points,' Celina conceded. 'But I'd have given the moon to go somewhere to stay. To me a holiday wasn't a holiday unless you slept in a hotel and woke up somewhere different.'

'They were probably the same seagulls,' he pointed out, raising a smile.

'It was always the same sun too,' Celina told him. 'But people still flocked in their thousands to the Mediterranean and other warmer climes.'

'And generated concrete jungles no discerning holidaymaker could possibly want to stay in. I don't suppose they've ruined Southport, have they?'

'No, thank goodness. Blackpool's much more commercialised. Southport's more like Bournemouth or Eastbourne, a retirement resort, although there have been a few developments recently, aimed at families with young children, not teenagers out for a few thrills and a good time. And that's not knocking Blackpool. I've had many a happy day there. It's all good, clean fun if you go to enjoy yourself.'

'Lots of white-knuckle rides and candy-floss and toffee-apples?' he asked.

Celina nodded. 'And fish and chips and popcorn, and, believe it or not, oysters.'

'I can believe it. It's a seaside resort, and that and fishing go more or less hand in hand. But oysters are one of the delicacies you didn't bother with, I take it?'

Celina shuddered. 'Urgh! Nasty, slimy things. It makes my blood go cold just thinking about them.'

'And how often have you tried them?' he enquired.

Celina looked sheepish. 'They always looked so offputting,' she confessed lamely as Luke laughed.

Dinner wasn't quite the strain Celina had been anticipating but, even so, she was more than a little glad when their taxi dropped them off at the hotel just a little after midnight. Luke suggested a nightcap, but Celina shook her head.

'I've had enough,' she said. 'Two glasses of wine and I'm halfway to being tipsy; three and I'm under the table.'

'Have a fruit juice, then, or a Coke,' Luke urged, and Celina, hesitating, found herself propelled across to the bar.

They found a corner table and sat down, Celina already beginning to regret not having gone straight up. It had been a long day, a bit of an up-and-down day, and she was tired. She smothered a yawn. Luke sat close, adding to her feelings of unease.

'I'm not making things easy for you, am I, Celina?'

'What do you mean?' she asked, turning her body slightly to face him.

Luke's fingers curled around the balloon of his glass and he swirled the golden liquid round and round before taking a sip. 'I'm not being fair. I talked you into this marriage for reasons of my own and I'm not sticking to my side of the bargain.'

'I don't remember signing a bride's charter,' Celina replied, trying to remain calm and beginning to wish for a brandy.

'No, but that doesn't entitle me to take advantage of the situation.'

'Look, Luke, I'm a big girl now and you're wrong. I came into this with both eyes open. I knew what I was doing, and, believe me, if I don't like something I'll say so.'

'Does that mean you're not regretting it?' he asked, the quiet words sending a chill of fear to her heart.

'I'm not,' she answered calmly, far more calmly than she felt. 'Are you?'

Unexpectedly he smiled and the feeling of doom disappeared. 'No, Celina. The set-up suits me fine and I should have known you'd have the sense to say so if you wanted out.'

'No, I've never been backwards at coming forwards,' she found herself saying lightly, treating him to a taste of northern pithiness.

'So you'll tell me when you are,' he persisted, though the smile remained on his face.

'Luke, I won't be the one who gets fed up, I promise you that. I'm the one getting the bargain, not you, whatever your feelings on the subject. And it's early days yet. Heavens, we've only been married thirty-six hours. Ask me how I feel in another two weeks, two months, two years—if we get that far. And when *you* want out that's when I'll want out. It's as simple as that.'

'If only it were,' he replied solemnly.

'Stop looking for problems,' she told him, patting his hand. 'Life's complicated enough without creating imaginary bugbears.'

'Quite the philosopher, aren't you?' he observed, though not unkindly. 'Life's dished out more than its fair share of knocks to you and yet you keep bouncing back. Your mother, your father, and now Danny.'

'Do all our conversations have to come back to him?' Celina asked, slightly irritated. 'Danny's over and done with. I've married you. Good grief, if I didn't know you better I'd suspect a touch of old-fashioned jealousy. Can't we forget Danny?'

'Hardly.' Luke's lips twitched. 'He is my brother, he was your fiancé, and sooner or later we have to go back and face him.'

'He made his decision,' Celina pointed out, 'and we made ours. Danny can hardly object.'

'No, I suppose not. But I guess I feel responsible somehow. I could have talked him into staying, into facing you at least, and who knows? You might have sorted things out, could even have come to Paris with Danny instead of me.'

It was a sobering thought: Danny at her side, Danny's laughter in her ears, Danny's infectious sense of humour filling her with fun. How much easier life would have been with Danny, a carousel of frivolity and excitement, and how empty, too, without the one ingredient that made all marriages worthwhile—love.

Love! Celina started visibly. It wasn't possible. The whole idea was ludicrous, absurd. She couldn't love Luke—could she? And yet it explained such a lot. Her antagonism, her sense of unease, her unconscious need for his approval. She glanced up. Luke was watching her carefully, his eyes dark, his expression unfathomable, and Celina's heart turned a somersault in her breast. She loved him! How could she not have known?

'I've no regrets,' she told him, voice not quite steady as she returned his gaze unblinkingly.

'Good. This hasn't been wasted, then.' He reached into an inside pocket, drawing out a small square packet. 'It's my wedding gift to you,' he explained, taking her hand, placing the beautifully giftwrapped parcel on her upturned palm. 'Go on, open it. It won't bite.'

She loosened the wrappings and then hesitated again before opening the box, her eyes darting to his, seeking reassurance.

A smile hovered about his lips.

Taking a deep breath, Celina pressed the tiny catch and the lid flicked open. 'Oh!' she gasped, and then she halted, stunned. The large oval sapphire with its garland of diamonds glinted up from its velvet cushion.

Luke took hold of her left hand. 'May I?' he asked, lifting the ring from its nest, the facets catching the light, dazzling Celina with their brilliance.

She nodded, her vision beginning to blur from the tears which hovered on her lashes.

With slow, steady movements Luke slipped the ring on to her wedding finger, sliding it easily over the knuckle and into place beside the plain gold band he had placed there less than two days before.

'It's beautiful, Luke,' Celina whispered, too choked to continue, and as the tears spilled over, scalding her cheeks, she caught his expression: surprise, concern, perplexity, and finally a dawning, doubting comprehension before his arms reached out, drawing her into his embrace, holding her to him, cocooning her in the warmth and safety of his body.

CHAPTER SIX

LATER Celina had laughed it off. 'It was such a surprise and such a beautiful present,' she told him the following morning when they'd both slept late and were enjoying a leisurely breakfast in their room. 'And I guess I was tired. It had been a long day, with the wedding and everything the day before; my emotions simply ran away with me. I never realised I had it in me.'

Luke had shrugged. 'It's only a ring, Celina,' he'd pointed out offhandedly. 'An engagement ring. Most married women wear one, after all, so why not you?'

Celina had lowered her gaze, flushing, part of her pleasure in the gift evaporating. Luke was a rich man, no doubt used to giving expensive presents. It meant little to him and it would be embarrassing if Celina made too much of it.

The incident served to put her on her guard, though. She'd come very close to giving herself away, and Luke was no fool. She'd have to be careful in future. Their strange bargain suited them both, as long as there were no emotional ties. It wasn't a marriage Luke wanted, but a partnership. He'd be horrified if he ever suspected the truth, and she knew she couldn't afford a repeat performance of such an emotional scene, couldn't afford any slip-ups. It wasn't going to be easy, but then, she hadn't expected that it would be.

They spent another three days in Paris before they moved on, heading south, stopping where the fancy took them, visiting châteaux, touring vineyards, exploring interesting villages and towns. It was a carefree time for them both, Celina remembering to act her part, Luke such good company that he made it easy for her.

There were no moonlight kisses or awkward bedroom scenes, and, though she knew deep down that it was safer that way, the demon in her could only mourn their absence. For the most part, though, common sense continued to rule.

They arrived back in London on a typically English day—grey and overcast with a hint of drizzle—and Celina's spirits sank. The honeymoon was over—literally—and real life was about to intrude, except that, as far as her life with Luke went, she wasn't sure where the reality began. She was like a character in a play, immersed in a brand new role, still struggling to learn her lines; only there weren't any lines, just disconcerting ad libs which gave few clues to the unfolding scenario. She was, to coin a phrase, playing it by ear.

And London, too, had something else that hadn't yet intruded: Maressa Majors, footloose, fancy-free, and back to claim her prize—Luke. Except that Luke was suddenly not available. An awful thought occurred then, banished at once but lingering in the dark recesses of her mind. It was the perfect punishment, the perfect revenge. Luke, parading his new wife for all the world to see, Maressa included. Until he decided to explode the carefully constructed fiction, put an end to the empty shell of their marriage—leaving him free also. Far-fetched though it seemed, it explained such a lot, and, though Celina didn't want to believe it, she was horribly afraid that she did.

Their taxi dropped them at Luke's apartment—*their* apartment now, she supposed—and Celina ran a nervous tongue over taut, dry lips. They were home. She stood in silence beside him as the lift whisked them upwards, stealing occasional panicky glances at his set profile. Not one for idle chatter, he'd seemed to withdraw more and more into himself over the past hour, and Celina wondered what was going on inside his head. Nothing very pleasant, intuition told her as a shiver ran down her spine. They were home all right, but just how long it would continue to be their home—together—was anybody's guess.

The lift doors swung open and they stepped out into the deep pile of the carpet. Luke turned his head then, piercing blue eyes reaching the very soul of her, turning her legs to jelly, and, as if sensing her unease, he smiled reassuringly.

'Welcome home, Mrs Sinclair,' he murmured, dropping the two large suitcases and moving so swiftly towards her that Celina had no time at all to fathom his intentions. He swung her up into his arms confidently, easily, her slender seven and a half stones seemingly weightless, and, pushing open the apartment door, carried her over the threshold.

'Luke!' Celina protested laughingly, half alarmed, half excited, totally bewildered. 'Put me down.'

'All part of the tradition of bringing home the bride,' he explained with a mischievous twinkle, running the back of his hand down and across her cheek in an unexpected gesture of affection. Celina felt herself tremble, her eyes filling up with tears, Luke's face swimming before her as she took an unsteady step backwards, but, even as she moved, Luke's arm slid down, catching at her shoulder, halting her.

'Hey! No need for that,' he whispered huskily, dipping his head, kissing away the salty trickle of her tears. He drew back slightly, eyes smoky, smouldering, enquiring; the spark igniting, flaring, consuming. As Luke's arms moved round, pulling her into his body, a powerful surge of desire ran through her. For one fleeting imaginary moment she held back, going rigid at his touch, and then her heart took over. She melted against him, her mouth opening under his, moving against his, welcoming his tongue. She inhaled the faint but distinctive aroma of his Aramis aftershave, was aware of his hands sliding down her back, resting on her buttocks, tugging her nearer and nearer, joining her body to his, the very power of his taut muscles exciting her, engulfing her.

His hands moved upwards, cradling her tiny waist, and Celina pushed her body further into his, unconsciously signalling her need of him. The hands moved on, caressing, stroking, exciting, and Celina found herself swaying against him as long, sensuous, sensitive fingers brushed the swell of her breasts. She arched her back, instinctively allowing his hands to slip round, to close around them, and moaned aloud at the bitter-sweet needles of pleasure that darted through her body.

The kiss went on, deeper and deeper, and Celina was drowning in his arms, drowning under the urgent pressure of his lips on hers.

When finally he drew away she slumped in disappointment against him, confused, unfulfilled, yet aware of his ragged breathing, and her spirits soared again. He hadn't been indifferent, his body had responded, had given him away. Luke had wanted her every bit as much as she had wanted him, and yes, this time she *had* wanted him, hadn't wanted him to stop. She had forgotten for the moment that he didn't love her. It didn't matter. She loved him. That was enough. She raised her face to his, wanting so much to tell him that she loved him, wanted him, wanted him so badly that it hurt.

Their eyes locked, full of love and wonder, and Celina parted her lips, the words she needed to tell him on the tip of her tongue; and then the scene slipped, dissolved, the tender lines of passion on his face disintegrating so quickly that Celina thought she must have imagined it all. Luke returned her gaze, unblinking, eyes dark, unreadable. He stepped away from her.

'Let's get these inside,' he said briskly, killing the moment of magic.

She followed him in silence, carrying the smallest and lightest of the cases. Luke paused in the doorway of a bedroom.

'You can have this one,' he told her. 'I'll sleep next door.'

He left her to unpack, and Celina slumped on the bed, tears of frustration threatening. She controlled herself with difficulty, taking deep, calming breaths, determined that not a single tear would fall. She didn't understand him. He had wanted her every bit as much as she had wanted him and yet he'd drawn back, denied her, rejected her. She closed her eyes, remembering clearly that other time in Paris, their wedding night, when things had gone so disastrously wrong. He had wanted her then too, and had mistaken her reluctance. She smiled grimly. His idea of revenge was an apt one.

When she was a little calmer she gazed around. It was a strange sensation, seeing her new home for the very first time, but, if first impressions were anything to go by, Celina was reassured. She could alter what she wanted, Luke had informed her earlier, but if this room was indicative of the rest of the apartment she'd be changing very little.

The bedroom was large—the master bedroom? she wondered, liking the feeling of space created by the soft bronze mirrors of the wardrobe which covered an entire wall and stretched from floor to ceiling. It had a vaguely oriental feel, rattan, bamboo and black lacquer happily co-existing, and, though unusual, was warm and welcoming. Her mouth twisted into a tight smile. A lot more welcoming than its owner, she admitted wryly.

She turned her attention to her luggage. Luke had insisted that she bought extra suitcases. Her collection of clothes hadn't quite expanded to fill them but she could see his point. She unpacked the articles likely to crease most, and her nightclothes. A new nightdress had been one of her early acquisitions, a full-length, high-necked,

Victorian-style cotton nightie suitable for the most prudish of prudes, not that it would matter now if Luke was sleeping in another room.

On impulse she put it away, dragging out the unused one. There still wasn't a lot to it, but that didn't matter either. Luke might consider her sexless but that didn't mean she had to live up to his image. She'd wear it, and damn Luke! It would make her feel better, and that was the important thing.

Finally she wandered out, her nose following the appetising aroma of sizzling bacon. Pausing on the threshold of the kitchen, she realised just how hungry she was. Lunch had been a sandwich on the plane and seemed half a lifetime away.

'Need a hand?' she asked, leaning back against the doorpost.

Luke turned his head. He had been flipping bacon and tomatoes under the grill and hadn't heard her approach.

'Thanks. The dining-room's through there.' He nodded. 'You can lay the table: cutlery in the end drawer, napkins in the middle. How do you like your eggs?' he asked as Celina moved away.

'Well done, please, sunny-side up,' she replied, crossing to the open doorway.

'There's a freezerful of food,' Luke told her once they were sitting at the table enjoying their meal. 'Mrs Wilson's a treasure, a first-rate cook, but I thought you might enjoy a bit of good old British fare now that we're back in England.'

'Mrs Wilson?' Celina queried.

'My housekeeper—our housekeeper,' he corrected. 'She comes in every day apart from weekends. She's going to get a shock when she hears about you. Don't worry,' he added, sensing her reaction. 'You'll hit it off fine. She's been trying to marry me off for years so you're a definite plus in her eyes.'

Celina swallowed a smile. She wasn't too sure about that, but she let the comment pass, turning her attention back to her food.

'This is lovely,' she told him between mouthfuls. 'One of my favourite meals. I used to spoil myself on Sundays and have the lot for breakfast: bacon, sausages, tomatoes, mushrooms, hash-browns, and then I'd be a real glutton and finish up with toast and marmalade.'

'It's a wonder you didn't explode,' Luke observed. 'How on earth did you keep your weight down?'

'Easy, really. On weekdays I didn't eat breakfast at all, and on Sundays it was breakfast and lunch combined, with a salad for tea, and in between I'd walk off all the calories.'

'You went walking?'

'Of course. Don't look so surprised. Back home I was a member of a rambling club, but that lapsed once I came to London. Still, I did try to get as much fresh air as possible, and even in London there was always the zoo or the parks.'

'Alone?'

'Usually, though sometimes with Anita. It really wasn't Danny's scene. He thought I was crackers.'

'I bet he did. Danny's idea of walking was the ten yards between the front door and the parked car, and he'd have done away with that if it weren't for the flowerbeds.'

Celina giggled. 'I don't think we had a great deal in common, really,' she observed, totally without thinking.

'That's not what I heard from Danny,' Luke slipped in, deceptively mildly.

'Oh? And what exactly had you heard?' Celina asked, alarm bells jangling out a warning in her head. They'd have to broach the subject of Danny sooner or later, she knew that, but there were probably better moments than their first night back in London.

Luke wiped his mouth and placed the crumpled napkin on the table. He leaned back in his chair, eyes narrowing as they focused on Celina, lips set into a hard, thin line.

Celina watched with curious fascination. His shirt was open at the neck and she could see the dark shadow of hair that she knew was only the periphery of the mass that covered his chest.

'Come, now, Celina, you don't expect me to repeat my brother's more raunchy descriptions of your relationship, surely? Wouldn't want to embarrass the lady, now, would we?' he sneered, making Celina's blood run cold.

'Innuendo's cheap enough,' she countered, voice carefully neutral. It didn't matter what he said, Celina knew the truth and lies couldn't hurt her. She met his gaze, holding his eyes with her own, determined not to give way to him.

'But not you, apparently.'

Luke's words sank in. 'I beg your pardon?' she asked, still not blinking.

'You set a high price, Celina. You had Danny in the palm of your hand and, the more he gave, the more you took, the more you wanted. What would have happened when the money ran out? And it would have done, the way things were going. What would you have done with Danny then—traded him in for a richer man, another susceptible victim?' he asked, deceptively mildly.

Celina swallowed hard, hearing the words but unable to sort out any meaning. 'I've told you before, Luke, I don't know what you're talking about.'

'Don't you really?' he enquired in the same bland tone. 'That's what you'd like me to believe, isn't it? Quite the accomplished actress, but you don't fool me. I'm not Danny and I can see right through your clever little ploys. You even kept your job—nice touch, that, hanging on to your independence. Danny thought it was wonderful. But that wasn't the real reason, was it?' he asked, voice hardening with every word. 'No!' he snarled. 'You *thought* you'd hooked him, but just in case he got away there was always the job to fall back on. Till the next mug came along. And, while poor Danny was singing your praises, you were taking his money, bleeding him dry, taking him for every penny. So——' he paused, pinning her with his eyes, his entire face sneeringly contemptuous '—where's it all gone?'

'Don't ask me,' Celina protested, more stunned than angry. 'Ask Danny.'

'And listen to even more lies while Danny covers up for you? Oh, no,' Luke rasped. 'This time I want the truth, and you, madam, are going to provide it.'

'In that case, Luke, you're going to have a long, long wait.'

'Wrong, Celina. Patience never was my strong point, and as far as you're concerned it ran out ten minutes ago. You've fleeced Danny; you know it and I know it. The only question now is what have you done with it all? You haven't spent it on yourself, that's pathetically obvious, and yet the money's gone somewhere, hasn't it, Celina? Hasn't it?'

'I don't believe I'm hearing this.'

Luke laughed, a chilling, mirthless sound. 'I bet you don't. Clever, clever Celina overlooked one very important detail—me. *I* control Danny's financial affairs and shall do for another three years. And when he came cap in hand and full of excuses, the same old dreary excuses, I wasn't a bit surprised. Except that this time it was different, this time he really had lost his head, this time Danny was getting married—to you.'

'Ah, yes!' Celina jeered, stung into attacking. 'I think I'm beginning to see. Power mad, aren't you, Luke? *Controlling* Danny, controlling me, playing God. Gives you a thrill, doesn't it, arranging people's lives? Only Danny was getting away, slipping the shackles, es-

caping. Can't have little brother making his own decisions. Good grief, no! Creates a dangerous precedent.'

'Stick to the point, Celina. You might have dazzled
Danny with your clever use of words but it won't work
with me. Quit stalling. You'll have to tell me sooner or
later; it may as well be now.'

'If you wait for me, Luke, you'll wait forever. But,
since you obviously know so much about it, allow me
to make a suggestion. *You* tell me.'

'Shall I?' he asked, angling his head, piercing blue
eyes raking her face, needles of ice stabbing at the core
of her. 'Yes, why not?' he almost crooned. 'Why not
tell the little bitch exactly what I think, exactly what I
know?' He leaned back, balancing on the two back legs
of the chair, his eyes bottomless pools of hate. He
nodded, and then smiled evilly. 'Yes, Celina, since you've
asked, I'll tell you. There's a man. There has to be. It's
the only thing that makes any sense. And I should have
known, should have realised sooner, should have picked
up all the clues. I am right, aren't I?'

'You're mad,' Celina told him flatly. She reached for
the wine bottle, shaking fingers topping up her glass.
She took a long, hard drink before flicking her gaze back
across the table. 'You're mad,' she repeated in the same
toneless voice. 'Absolutely mad.'

'I'm not the one who's mad, Celina. That was Danny's
problem. Mad about you, mad enough to squander a
fortune on you. Men have lost their heads before—literally, some of them—over a woman, and I've often
wondered why. But now you can tell me.' He halted,
looking her up and down, slowly, deliberately,
insultingly. 'Well, Celina, are you going to explain? What
makes you so special? What have you got that Danny
simply couldn't do without—some new technique
perhaps that left him begging for more and more and
more?'

'Don't be so revolting,' Celina flashed, temper rising. 'I don't have to sit here and listen to this.'

'Yes, you do,' he barked. He swung forwards without warning, a fist crashing down on the table, adding terror to the words. 'Oh, yes, you do!'

Celina jumped, dropping her glass, which shattered on impact, the wine spreading out across the starched white cloth like an obscene bloodstain. She stared at it, immobile, frozen, and then reached out a tentative hand to gather the largest of the pieces.

'Leave it!' Luke commanded. 'And you're going nowhere, Celina, not yet, not until you've told me what I want to know.'

'Why?' she blazed. 'Where's the point? You're not going to believe anything I say, so why should I bother? Innocent until proven guilty—isn't that the essence of British law? Only not in this case, not where I'm concerned. That decision's already been made. Mr Luke Sinclair, the judge and the jury all rolled into one, has sat and reached a verdict. And you're so arrogant that you couldn't possibly be wrong. Of course not!' she jeered. 'That would be tantamount to admitting that you're not perfection personified. Can't have you shattering any illusions, can we, Luke, about you or Danny? The ego couldn't take it.'

'You're sidetracking, Celina; the issue isn't me or Danny. The subject under discussion is you.'

'Then, as far as I'm concerned, the subject is closed.' She began collecting plates together, hands still shaking, every fibre of her body taut with suppressed emotion.

'I disagree,' Luke growled. 'You can run away into the kitchen if it makes you feel any better, but I'll be right behind you every step of the way. I've only just started.'

'I don't have to listen,' she pointed out coldly. 'You can say the words, you can say what you like. You can recite Shakespeare, or Dickens, or the South London telephone directory for all I care. It doesn't mean I'll be listening.'

She stood up, the pile of plates and cutlery in her hands, and made to move past. Luke snatched the plates away, knocking the knives and forks on to the floor where they clattered and skidded under the table.

'Let me past,' she hissed, her own eyes twin pools of venom. 'Get out of my way.'

'Not until I've finished,' Luke spat. 'Not until I've had my say. I've been waiting for this moment and now you're going to listen to every word I say. You'll listen, you'll understand, and you won't forget. I *know*, Celina. I know you've taken Danny's money and I know you've married me for mine, but you won't get it. I've no intention of standing meekly to one side while you filter money from my account to someone else's. You can tell him—whoever he is—that his meal-ticket's cancelled. My wife, *my wife*,' he emphasised, 'is answerable to me, and my wife will no longer be subsidising someone else's pleasures. My wife will do as I say.'

'This is the nineteen-nineties, Luke,' Celina pointed out, not even angry any more. The accusations would be absurd if the grain of truth in them hadn't such a bitter flavour. 'I've still got my job and not a court in the land would support such an archaic viewpoint. You don't have to shower me with furs and expensive jewellery. I neither expect them nor want them. And as for money, well, I'm not asking for charity, just for what is mine by right, mine as your wife. If you want to withhold it, then that's your prerogative, but I don't have to accept the situation.'

'You're threatening me.'

'No, Luke, you're threatening me. I'm simply appealing to the better side of your nature—if you have one.'

'No, you little bitch, you're threatening me. Luke has to play ball or his scheming wife blasts the sordid details all over the front pages of the gutter Press.'

'And destroy us both, Luke? Have a bit of sense. I have my pride; heaven knows, it's probably all I do have.'

'And a reputation to protect as well, I suppose?' he jeered, his ugly, grating laugh echoing inside her head. 'All right, lady, you win—this time. I'll fulfil my side of the bargain down to the very last penny. But be warned: I'll be watching you, and the first hint I get that you're misappropriating my money I'll be down on you so hard that you won't know what's hit you.'

He did a swift about-turn and strode off, leaving Celina alone in the dining-room. A few minutes later she heard the slamming of a door. He'd gone out.

She sank down into the nearest chair, her entire body shivering uncontrollably. She sat on for a full ten minutes, her mind a jumble of words and emotions. Eventually she roused herself and, with movements slow and weary, started to clear away some of the mess.

She put the soiled cloth to soak in a bowl of cold water, and finished loading plates and cutlery in the dish-washer. She was numb. Her body was chilled, her mind anaesthetised, and her movements were purely auto-matic. She measured the coffee into the percolator, counting each spoonful twice before her brain was sat-isfied that she had the right mix.

She wanted a brandy but had no idea of where to look, and a cursory search of the kitchen cupboards yielded nothing alcoholic at all. She remembered the wine they'd had with their meal and wondered where Luke kept it, and, thinking of Luke, began to crumple inside.

How he must hate her. That hurt most. Not his con-tempt, his high-handed attitude, his sneering accu-sations. Just the naked hatred. And he was wrong, yet right and wrong at the same time, too near the truth for his words not to leave a lasting impression. And she *had* taken money from Danny, but nothing like the amount Luke was implying. Three months' advance fees for the nursing home, a few thousand pounds, which Danny, being Danny, had refused to accept when Celina had tried to pay it back. Then, when she'd thought of a way she could return it, they'd decided to get married, and once they'd started making plans for a life together the money had ceased to be important. Her lips twisted bitterly. How ironic. She couldn't explain it all to Luke now, and if she did she doubted that he'd listen, let alone understand.

She finished the tidying up, restored the kitchen and dining-room to pristine perfection, and then stood very still in the middle of the floor, hugging her arms to her body, more alone than she'd ever been and suddenly lost for something to do. She glanced at her watch. Luke had been gone little more than an hour, though it seemed much longer, and Celina tried to imagine the sort of mood he'd be in when he got home. If he bothered coming home. It was all too easy to picture him spending the night elsewhere, another apartment, another woman for company, another bed... She squeezed her eyes tightly together, trying to block out the vision, loathing the image that sprang to mind and yet caught fast in awful fascination as the pictures ran on and on unchecked, tormenting, punishing.

Finally she brushed away the tears, rousing herself from her lethargy. She headed back to her bedroom, choosing to unpack the rest of her things, not wanting to sit idle, thinking, waiting, and then decided to make use of Luke's continued absence to explore her new home.

It was beautiful, breathtaking, each room a whole new source of delight, and Celina knew instinctively that she could be happy there. As long as Luke didn't decide to keep on punishing her with his biting accusations, she could be happy there. Reaching the last of the bedrooms, she paused on the threshold. Luke's cases were still stacked on the floor and Celina registered automatically that the bed was unmade. It took a few moments for the reason to sink in. Of course, Mrs Wilson wasn't expecting visitors. She had, naturally enough, made up only one bed.

She found the airing cupboard and rooted about for pillow-slips and sheets. It would give her something to do, fill some time, but the task was soon over and then she was at another loose end.

She wanted to do something, anything; anything that would keep her mind away from Luke's words. That so much was simply not true didn't take away the sting of them. And he hated her. She could take everything else, but not his hatred.

Choking back tears, she went to find her book. She would read. Many a time she had lost herself in a good book, but tonight, of course, the words on the page refused to attract her attention. She curled up on the settee in the smaller of the lounges, postponing thoughts of bed till Luke returned. *If* he returned . . . She glanced at her watch again. It was past twelve. Where on earth had he got to?

She poured another coffee, hugging the drink to her, extracting warmth from the cup between her hands, and then she turned back to the novel. By the time she'd read the same page five times over without taking in a single word she gave up. Hooking a stray lock of hair back behind an ear, she stood and stretched, moving over to the window, parting the curtains to look out at the night, gazing unseeingly at the twinkling lights of the city.

She moved aimlessly about the room, fingering this ornament, straightening that. In one corner, on top of a bookcase, was a photograph. The smiling couple stared out at her, the woman's features so strikingly familiar that Celina knew without a doubt that it was Luke's mother, with, she guessed, his stepfather. How happy they seemed, a stab of pain running through her at the thought. Happy. Such a nice, understated, undervalued state of mind.

She replaced the photograph and returned to the settee, the eyes in the picture seeming to follow her across the room. She checked the time again, a small, worried frown furrowing her brow. She wished he'd come home. And then she heard a noise, the soft whirr of the lift. She held her breath, listening for a key in the lock, footsteps echoing on the polished tiles of the hallway, and she fixed her eyes on the closed door, willing him to enter, wanting so much to see him before they went to bed, taking their anger with them, and yet just as afraid that the heated words would flare up again more intensely. The door swung open, Luke's body filling the frame, his expression one of surprise.

'I thought you'd forgotten where you lived.' Celina recovered her composure first.

'And I thought you'd be asleep by now,' Luke replied quietly.

'I got involved with my book. Didn't notice the time,' she lied, closing it quickly.

'Any coffee going?' he asked, nodding at her cup.

Celina uncurled herself. 'I'll heat some up,' she said, moving through to the kitchen. It didn't take long, and she put two cups on the tray before carrying it back, placing it on the small occasional table between the settee and the armchair.

Luke took the chair and Celina sat opposite, a little wary of him now that he was actually back in the flesh. She watched him from underneath her lashes. He looked tired, strained, and she wanted to reach out and run her fingers across his forehead, smooth away the worry-lines. Luke glanced at her quickly, catching her off guard.

She flushed, glancing away, nerves tingling at the charged atmosphere. She began to wish she hadn't waited up after all, had given the anger and antagonism time to die down overnight.

She didn't know where she was again. They'd come so far, were friends almost, and suddenly one chance remark had plunged them back to the beginning, hating one another, blaming each other. At least, Luke hated *her*.

It didn't seem fair. But what could she say? She couldn't tell him the truth, it would only reinforce his view of her, and yet unless she offered some defence he could only carry on thinking the worst of her. She couldn't win. Whatever she did, she couldn't win. But she had to do something to temper his contempt.

'Luke,' she began hesitantly, the fingers of one hand nervously tugging at the material of her dress.

'Celina?'

'It isn't what you think, Luke,' she pleaded softly, eyes deep, troubled pools.

'Leave it, Celina.'

'I can't. Not like this.'

'Guilty conscience?' he asked, pinning her with the intensity of his gaze.

Celina blenched. He'd hit the nail right on the head again, but he was wrong as well as right, and obviously not in the mood to listen, to even try to understand.

She dropped her eyes, sealing her guilt, self-pity welling up, threatening to swamp her. Swallowing hard, she stood up, the lines of her body weary and dejected. 'I'll go to bed, then,' she said quietly, moving woodenly to the door.

Luke's harsh laugh followed her. 'That's right, Celina,' he jeered cruelly. 'Go to bed. Run away and hide. I'll catch up with you, one day.'

CHAPTER SEVEN

IT WAS a relief to get back to work. Luke had raised an eyebrow when Celina had repeated her intention of keeping her job, but he had said nothing and Celina had let out an inaudible sigh of relief, glad they weren't about to fall out again so soon after arriving back in London. Besides, there was no earthly reason why she shouldn't work. True, Luke paid her an allowance that put her salary firmly in the shade, but, money aside, it was Celina's company that Luke wanted, and her organisational skills. Mrs Wilson kept the apartment spotless and continued to provide a first-class evening meal. Free from the drudgery of housework, Celina easily combined the roles of social hostess and librarian, donning her mantle as Luke's wife along with the elegant clothes that he insisted she must acquire, slipping effortlessly into her allotted part, sparkling and smiling, surprised at how easy it seemed and, surprisingly too, enjoying it. At home, alone with Luke, the atmosphere was more constrained. Out in company, she found she didn't need to make a conscious effort at all; she really did enjoy being with Luke and had to keep reminding herself that it was only a part she was playing and that sooner or later it would have to come to an end. Keeping herself as busy as possible pushed the gloomy threads of reality into the background. Time enough to face that when it finally arrived.

Being back in London had brought Maressa Majors back into focus. Celina had spent a nail-biting few weeks, expecting Luke to arrive home at any moment announcing that the marriage was over, but as the time passed and their lives slipped into some sort of recognisable routine Celina began to relax slightly. It was still there at the back of her mind that Luke had deliberately set the situation up, had married Celina in a calculated attempt to pay Maressa back for her defection, but in the absence of any real proof she could only try not to let the idea affect her. In any case, time would tell.

Luke, she discovered, worked hard too—quite an eye-opener. He'd once told her that he enjoyed work, but Celina had taken the comment with a pinch of salt as she'd gained the impression from Danny that Luke's varied business interests ran themselves, that Luke provided the backing but was purely a figurehead, content to take a back-seat role. It didn't take long to change that opinion, and she wondered how many more of Danny's pronouncements were only loosely based on fact.

She had been apprehensive about meeting Danny, discovering from Luke on the last day of their holiday that he was back too and, having been told about their marriage, was delighted for them both. But, by fair means or foul, they seemed destined not to meet. Mentioning Danny's name casually over dinner one evening, Celina was amazed at the change in atmosphere. Luke's features had frozen as he'd registered Celina's suggestion.

'Invite Danny over for a meal? What on earth for?' he had enquired frigidly, and Celina had hastily mumbled something about family commitments, tripping over her words, becoming more and more incoherent under the glassy glare of Luke's eyes. It wasn't a suggestion she chose to repeat, meekly accepting Luke's assurances that Danny was fine but was busier than usual and would 'drop by when he had the time'. Celina guessed that the brothers weren't exactly on the best of terms, and, suspecting herself as the reason, was glad to let the subject drop.

'Is that library of yours short-staffed?' Luke enquired one morning over breakfast.

'I don't think so. Why?' Celina replied, wondering what had prompted such a strange enquiry.

'You never seem to take time off. I thought you were entitled to an afternoon off occasionally, but you don't appear to bother. Leastways, you never seem to arrive home any earlier.'

'So?' Celina shrugged, beginning to feel just a shade uneasy.

'Idle curiosity, I suppose,' Luke replied, his eyes holding hers for a moment. 'You obviously don't need the money, so I guess you're not working all the hours God sends.'

'No.' Celina's heart began to thump uncomfortably in her breast. She hoped they weren't heading for another confrontation. She remembered all too clearly the last occasion money had been mentioned, on their first night back in England, and she didn't want any more heated words and wild accusations destroying their carefully constructed calm.

'So you do take time off?' Luke persisted, crumpling his napkin into a ball and placing it on the table in front of him.

'Yes, Luke. Thursdays.' Today, in fact, Celina acknowledged silently, and inwardly squirming under the direct gaze.

'And so what do you do with yourself, then?'

Celina flushed, realising she was being backed into a corner, alarm bells ringing loud and clear inside her head. Guilty conscience, she realised, at the same time beginning to resent Luke's not unnatural interest. She found herself on the defensive, unable to tell the truth, and assuming, wrongly, that Luke had reached his own conclusions.

'What is this, Luke?' she demanded, the edge to her voice clearly detectable. 'The grand Inquisition?

Checking up on my movements? I haven't seen Danny for weeks now, not since before we were married, in fact, but you don't really need me to tell you that, do you? After all, you employ him, you should be able to keep track of his movements.'

'As you say, I'm aware of how Danny fills his time. What I'm curious to know is how you fill yours, or the small amount you actually allow yourself to take.'

'Perhaps I do what other young women do. Visit the beauty salon, the hairdresser, spend time at the shops, meet Anita for a gossip, take in an afternoon show.'

'Perhaps,' Luke mused. 'And perhaps not.'

'You *are* checking up on me,' Celina challenged, her colour rising with her anger. She had always known he was capable of having her followed but had never really thought that he would do it.

'Do I need to?' Luke asked, holding her gaze, the steely blue eyes far too knowing for Celina's peace of mind.

'You tell me,' she tossed back at him, tilting her chin in defiance.

There was a loaded pause, and Celina held her breath, wondering what was coming next, when unexpectedly Luke smiled, bringing his hand down on to the table and covering Celina's in a rare moment of contact which heightened her colour, quickened the blood in her veins.

'No, Celina, I don't need to. I know you too well to have to resort to those kind of tricks.'

'You didn't always feel that way,' Celina pointed out, though warmed by his words and the gentle pressure of his fingers.

'I didn't always know you as well as I do now,' he replied gravely.

Celina dropped her gaze, not wanting to read too much into what Luke was saying. It was all too easy at times to allow herself to hope, to dream, to believe in something that deep down she knew could never exist.

Luke's voice cut into her thoughts. 'If you're not busy next Thursday afternoon how about spending it with me?' he suggested.

Celina's eyes opened wide. 'Why?'

'Do I need a reason?' he parried, but carried on before she could reply. 'I thought it time we went house-hunting. The apartment is fine as a temporary measure, but Mother will be over in the New Year, and when she arrives for a visit it's usually a long one. We'll definitely need extra room. In any case, it's time we bought something bigger, something more permanent.'

'I didn't think our arrangement stretched to long-term commitments,' Celina observed.

An eyebrow rose. 'Given the present statistics on divorce,' he informed her, 'our "arrangement" will probably last as long as many other marriages, or don't you see it that way?'

Celina shrugged. 'I suppose so,' she agreed solemnly.

'But you're not holding out much hope, is that it?' he asked, piercing blue eyes pinning her, refusing to allow her to look away.

'It isn't really up to me, is it, Luke?' Celina countered, her heart beginning to race again.

'Isn't it?' He spoke very quietly, and she had to strain to catch the words. He seemed deadly serious but she couldn't take the risk. He could simply be playing games with her, and she was much too vulnerable to cope with that. There were times when they seemed so compatible, so totally suited that Celina was amazed. They'd a lot more in common than she'd ever thought possible: the same cosmopolitan taste in music; a love of modern art and ballet and the theatre; a passionate interest in literature, as well as almost identical favourite authors. It served to underline how much she loved him, how much she wanted to believe that they *did* have a future—together—to look forward to. It was castles in the air, but sometimes, just occasionally, she allowed herself to believe it. More often than not, though, common sense prevailed. Luke had never intended anything other than a temporary arrangement and Celina knew it. They'd go their separate ways once someone he loved came on the scene, and in the meantime she wasn't prepared to allow him to have fun at her expense. Besides, at the back of her mind loomed the biggest, blackest cloud on the horizon of their marriage: Maressa.

'I'm sorry,' she told him, pulling herself together. 'I've already got something on. The week after maybe.'

'No.' Luke shook his head. 'That's out for me. I've got a lot on for the next few weeks. Still, it's no real problem. I'll pick up some brochures. Perhaps when you've time you could browse through them, pick out any you like, and I'll arrange for us to view. I would like to be settled in as soon as possible, especially with Christmas just around the corner. And, Celina,' he added brusquely, pushing back his chair as he rose to his feet, face dark and thunderous, 'you needn't worry. A new house doesn't bind you. You're free to go whenever you want to. Just let me know first, won't you, my dear?'

'Hello, Dad. How are you today?'

Francis Somerville was slumped in a wheelchair, eyes half closed, having forty winks, Celina guessed, forcing a smile but registering automatically the increased pallor of his skin.

The eyelids flickered open, her father's features lighting up with sudden, fleeting pleasure that caught at Celina's heart and triggered insidious stirrings of guilt. She should come more often. There was only her job standing in the way, and she didn't need to cling to that now, thanks to Luke. She'd be sorry to lose it, of course, enjoying the challenge of work, enjoying meeting people, but, with the size of allowance Luke made, she could afford to give it up, to spend more time here with her father. Luke didn't know it, but he'd lifted a burden from her shoulders. The nursing-home fees were only a part of the problem, albeit a big part, and yet, again thanks to Luke, that was one worry less.

'Hello, lass,' her father croaked, rousing himself.

Celina sat down on the bed, facing him, sharp eyes running the length of him. He seemed even thinner, if that were possible, and she was suddenly afraid. He'd come through so much, though his progress had been slow, pitifully slow at times, but these past few weeks there had been a change; less energy, less lucidity, less brightness in his eyes.

It reminded Celina of the dark times when her father's life had hung in the balance, and later when he'd lost the will to live. Celina had fought tooth and nail to give it back to him, to lift his burden of guilt. She hoped he wasn't slipping back, remembering, blaming himself. She chattered on, attempting to engage his attention, trying to rouse him from his lethargy. He *would* get better; she'd make sure he did.

Luke would never know how close to the truth he'd come, his accusations about a man in her life uncannily accurate, and yet, at the same time, so far wide of the mark as to be almost farcical. She wondered what his reactions would be if he ever did find out. Pity for a sick old man, or contempt for one of life's casualties? Compassion? Understanding? Or blame? She swallowed a sigh. She could well imagine. So many others had turned their backs, hadn't even tried to understand. And, if Francis Somerville's family could despise him, why should a stranger be different?

It had been a nightmare, and even now, three years later, Celina could still feel the pain of it. It had been a tangled story. The small family firm where her father had worked since leaving school had been threatened with closure, so he'd masterminded a plan whereby the work-force had bought the company out, raiding savings accounts, taking out bank loans, 'begging, borrowing and stealing', almost, to make it possible.

Celina, too, had played a part. Her mother had left her some money, quite a substantial amount, and Celina had insisted that her father made use of it. It belonged to them both as far as she was concerned, and this seemed a good way of investing it. Rather reluctantly her father agreed, this injection of cash just the impetus needed to get the scheme off the ground. And it worked, for a time. There were minor problems, but nothing that couldn't be handled, and everything seemed firmly set on course for success. Until interest rates started soaring, tying up more and more cash in repayments, cutting off investments, strangling the fledgling firm. And when it finally collapsed, Francis Somerville blamed himself.

A lot of people lost money, none more than Celina and her father, but it was his idea and his fault that everyone else was suffering, and nothing could convince him otherwise. Heartbroken, riddled with guilt and hounded by all the adverse publicity, he took the only course of action he'd seen left: suicide. He swallowed a mixture of pills, leaving a poignant note of explanation for Celina, but by sheer chance he was found in time and rushed to hospital.

But then, of course, the story broke, was front-page news in the local paper. Except that somehow the suicide *attempt* was reported as *reality*. The subsequent apology, printed a week or two later, was tucked away on the inside pages and was hardly worth the cost of the ink and two inches of column it occupied. Not surprising, really, that Luke had been misinformed.

The afternoon drew out, Celina pushing her father round the gardens, sitting for a while in a sheltered, sunny spot. He said little, adding to her unease. He didn't find it easy to talk at the best of times, the stroke leaving him partially paralysed, making everything he did such an effort. It all seemed so unfair at times that Celina could hardly believe it. Why should it have happened? Hadn't her father suffered enough? Hadn't he already paid the price—and more?

Finally, afraid her father would catch a chill, she took him back inside, and made them both a hot drink in the communal kitchen. The more mobile patients helped themselves, retaining a degree of independence, and Celina never ceased to be glad that the home she'd chosen for her father allowed as normal a life as possible in the circumstances. As far as the staff were concerned, the residents were people first and patients second.

By the time she'd washed and dried the cups and returned to say goodbye, her father had fallen asleep, his head nodding on his shoulder. Celina stood and watched him, a mixture of emotions gripping her.

'Bye, Dad,' she whispered, tiptoeing across the room. As she reached the door there was a soft rap on the wooden panel and the door swung slowly open. Celina recognised the tall, stooped figure at once, a long-stay patient in the room next door. 'Hello, Roger,' she greeted him. 'Come to see Dad? I've worn him out, I'm afraid. He's fast asleep. I hope he doesn't miss tea.'

'I'll keep an eye on him,' Roger replied. 'I'd forgotten it was Thursday. I thought I'd read him the paper for half an hour. He likes to keep up with the news. Still, never mind, I can come back later.' He hesitated a moment and then added, 'He's been a bit quiet these past few days, as if there's something on his mind. How did he seem to you?'

Celina caught the worried expression in Roger's eyes. He'd been good to her father, despite the two men's seeming to have little in common. Roger was a younger man, prematurely grey, the debilitating disease taking its toll on his body, laying waste his muscles but not impairing his mind. He spent long hours in a wheelchair but when he felt up to it managed to walk with the help of a frame.

With a shock she realised that he was probably about the same age as Luke, and the contrast between the two couldn't have been greater. 'Very quiet,' she acknowledged. 'Too quiet. I'll have a word with the doctor before I leave. Not that there's much she can do, not that there's much anyone can do, not really.' She glanced across at the sleeping form of her father and then back to Roger, standing, watching them both, velvet-brown eyes cloudy with concern. 'I'm glad you're here,' she said, raising a smile.

'I'll keep an eye on him,' he reassured her again. 'Try not to worry. It will all work out for the best, you'll see.'

Celina nodded. She really did hope so.

It was later than she expected when she arrived back, the rush-hour starting earlier than usual and quickly building up into a slow, frustrating crawl. Celina had slumped in the back of her taxi, glad of the chance to relax, and once again thankful that she'd resisted Luke's efforts to buy her a car of her own. She didn't see the point, not in a city like London where traffic was nose-to-tail for most of the day, and, besides, she'd got used to the underground now. Luke had been amazed at her refusal, the subsequent shrug of his shoulders more eloquent than words.

'Fine, Celina, if that's what you'd rather do. But the offer remains open for when you change your mind.'

Celina had simply smiled her thanks, not bothering to reply, knowing full well that it was highly unlikely that she would, and yet touched by Luke's concern. By way of a compromise she'd agreed that Luke could drop her off at work most mornings, allowing her to make her own way home at night.

The grandmother clock in the hallway chimed the hour as Celina inserted her key in the door. Six o'clock. Ninety minutes to shower and dress. They were dining out with clients, Luke had reminded her at breakfast, important clients, not that Celina felt up to it, not tonight.

She shrugged herself out of her coat, thoroughly weary, tossing it on her bed before moving through to the dining-room and pouring herself a small brandy with a very large Coke. She didn't normally touch alcohol so early in the evening, but tonight she definitely needed it.

She checked the Ansafone for messages, hoping against hope that Luke might have called, cancelling their evening, but there was nothing significant, just one or two queries for Luke which she duly stored in the memory before resetting the machine and wandering back to her bedroom. She toyed with the idea of a bath but decided she'd have trouble coaxing herself out once she got soaking, and reluctantly made do with a shower.

Slightly more refreshed, she wrapped herself in a bathrobe, towelling dry her hair before turning on the drier. She'd just take the edge off the dampness and then leave it to dry itself, knowing from experience that it would fall into soft, shining, natural-looking waves that would require only minimum attention before they went out. She reached for her bag, preferring the wide-toothed comb she carried around with her, and realised with a sigh of annoyance that she'd left it in the lounge.

Barefooted, she padded across just as the phone started ringing. Already pushed for time, she decided not to answer it and, not realising she had left the machine on 'talk', was already halfway back to the door when the husky tones of a woman's voice halted her.

'Luke, darling,' the woman drawled, raising the hairs on the back of Celina's neck, 'sorry I missed your call. I was beginning to think you'd forgotten I ever existed, but, there again, how could you?' A throaty laugh rang out and then she dropped her voice, the tone low and intimate. 'I've kept Saturday evening free, so I'll expect you then. Eight o'clock. And, Luke, don't bother

dressing, we'll eat in—Cantonese…your favourite.' She
ended with a smacking noise—a kiss, Celina deduced—
and didn't leave a name. But then, she didn't need to,
did she? Maressa Majors had made her opening move.

Feeling slightly queasy, Celina topped up her brandy.
The 'invitation' for Saturday didn't bother her. They
were already committed to the theatre and dinner, and
the people concerned were much too important to put
off at such short notice. But there were other evenings,
other Saturdays, times when Luke didn't need—or
want—Celina's company. With Maressa hovering in the
background, Celina had tried not to allow her imagination to run riot. So far she'd succeeded. But the next
time Luke went out without her…

She closed her eyes, squeezing back the tears. It wasn't
turning out to be the best of days and it wasn't over yet.
She glanced at her watch, horrified to discover that it
was almost seven and she was nowhere near ready.
Dashing away the tears, she made an effort to pull herself
together, making a bee-line for her bedroom and
careering full-tilt into Luke's solid form as she crossed
the hall.

'Whoa, there, lady,' he laughed deep in his throat,
catching hold, arms going round, holding her, steadying
her.

'L-Luke!' Celina stammered, cheeks flaming, caught
fast in his grip but caught fast too in the bottomless
depths of his twinkling blue eyes.

'Going somewhere?' he teased, making no effort at
all to release her.

'Yes, Luke.' She wriggled her way out of his grasp.
'As well you know. We're meeting the Danvers in less
than half an hour. At this rate I'll be going out half
dressed.'

'Oh, no, you won't,' he contradicted lightly, his gaze
running the length of her, not missing how the cotton
robe clung to still-damp contours. 'You'd bring London

to a standstill and get us both arrested. In any case, I've a much better idea.'

'Oh?' Celina queried, heart racing, cheeks an even deeper shade of crimson.

Luke nodded. 'Mm,' he murmured and then paused, deliberately provoking.

She swallowed her impatience, her gaze fastened on Luke's dancing eyes. They were late, *how* late was immaterial. It wasn't a trait Luke tolerated in others and she was surprised he was wasting valuable time now playing games.

The grandmother clock behind them started chiming. Celina glanced across, automatically checking the time against her wrist-watch. Some hint of what she was feeling must have registered on her face, for Luke smiled broadly.

'What would *you* like to do tonight?' he asked. 'Supposing you could do whatever you wanted? Be honest. You never know, someone with influence might just wave a magic wand.'

'I stopped believing in fairy-stories years ago,' Celina replied just a little bit tartly.

Luke raised a single reproving eyebrow. 'Tut! Tut!' he admonished lightly. 'You'll be telling me next that Santa doesn't exist. Well?'

Celina smiled, despite herself. 'What I'd really and honestly like to do most, given a completely free choice?' she asked, deciding to humour him.

Luke inclined his head. 'Just one wish, mind,' he cautioned.

'Well, in that case, here goes. Stay in, read a book, put my feet up, guzzle a glass of wine, and have a thoroughly lazy, thoroughly self-indulgent evening,' she told him, words tripping out without a pause. Then added mischievously, 'I never could count.'

Luke laughed, tossing back his head, the happy sound filling the hallway. 'Madam, you've the cheek of the devil,' he observed. 'But, if that's what you've asked for, then that is what you'll get—to the very letter.' And before she had time to react he'd picked her up, carried her off, laid her on the sofa, produced the book and the glass of wine, tucked a cushion under her legs and another behind her head. 'Another satisfied customer,' he murmured, taking himself off to shower and change. As he paused in the doorway he added, 'Give me five minutes and then I'll explain.'

As it turned out, Celina got exactly what she'd asked for. The Danvers had been forced to cancel at the last moment, and Luke seemed happy enough to fall in with Celina's plan.

Realising that they had the entire evening together, alone, she got dressed, slipping into jeans and T-shirt, feeling much too vulnerable clad only in her bathrobe. Besides, once Luke suggested sending out for a takeaway—Chinese, perhaps?—Celina received a painful jolt of reminder. Maressa Majors's message. She dawdled deliberately, giving Luke time to check the Ansafone, half expecting on her return that 'something important' would have turned up, demanding his immediate attention elsewhere.

She sipped her wine and studied his face surreptitiously, attempting to gauge his reaction, but he seemed relaxed enough and gradually, as the evening progressed, Celina relaxed too. If she was to worry about Maressa she'd worry herself into an early grave, and if it wasn't entirely a successful operation, banishing Maressa completely, at least it didn't dominate all her thoughts.

Tiring of her book, a trite tale of love and intrigue set against the backdrop of modern politics, she turned her attention to the *Guardian* Luke had just put down. Having read the news already, she folded it open at the crossword, occasionally asking Luke for an answer when she had some letters in place.

His interest roused, Luke moved across to the settee, where they could share the paper, his bent head unnervingly close to her own. The crossword built up, leaving only three to solve, but, despite their combined efforts, they were finally forced to concede defeat.

'Not that I would have got this far on my own,' he told her admiringly. 'I can cope with most of them but these alphabetical ones completely throw me. I don't know how you even begin to fit the answers on the grid.'

'Logic, Luke,' Celina preened. 'And mountains of patience. Just natural superiority, I guess you'd call it.'

He grinned good-naturedly. 'I'll argue that one another day,' he said as he ruffled her hair. 'Coffee?'

Celina shook her head. 'No, thanks. I'm tired. I think I'll turn in. I've got a heavy day tomorrow, so an early night will do me good.'

They exchanged goodnights and she took herself off, sliding into bed and snuggling under the duvet. She closed her eyes, expecting sleep, but after fifteen minutes of wrestling with the pillows she sat up again. Her tiredness had passed, giving way to feelings of vague dissatisfaction. Maressa Majors, she realised with sinking heart. She might have known. With a smothered groan she reached for the light. She wouldn't sleep now, not for a while, at any rate. She'd read. Half an hour of that uninspiring book should do the trick, but of course, she'd forgotten she'd left it in the lounge.

She pulled on her robe, not bothering to belt it since all was dark and quiet, and padded softly past Luke's closed door. 'Sweet dreams,' she murmured as she drew level, fervently hoping that Maressa wasn't dominating his thoughts too.

She didn't notice the slightly open door on her return, and started in surprise when Luke emerged from the bathroom, the sudden flash of light blinding her.

'Oh!' she shrieked, dropping her book and narrowly missing her bare toes. Automatically she bent to retrieve it, Luke having the same idea, and their heads collided, knocking her slightly off balance.

'Steady on,' Luke murmured, his hands cradling her shoulders.

It was a light and casual contact but it turned her knees to water, the warmth spreading out from his fingers like a flame licking through her. She rocked on her heels and came to rest, Luke's hands holding her steady.

She glanced up. He was watching her, his expression unreadable, but as his gaze swept over her, taking in the open robe, the flimsy nightdress beneath, the rise and fall of her full breasts clearly visible under the lace, she sensed a shudder run through his body, and the blood in her veins began to boil. With a primeval growl deep in his throat Luke swept her up, gathering her to him, holding her tight, so tight that Celina could hardly breathe. She raised her head and their eyes locked, the message in Luke's smouldering, igniting, fanning the flame in Celina's. An eternity passed in an instant, and then his mouth came down on hers and Celina knew that she was lost.

She was lifted up, cradled in his arms, carried as easily as a small child, and she relaxed against him, revelling in the expanse of chest under her cheek, drowning in the smell of him, the feel of him, the warmth of him against her body.

He paused for a moment at the foot of her bed, his eyes boring into hers, searching for something, until finally he nodded, apparently satisfied, placing her gently on the sheet before lying down beside her, drawing her into his arms.

'I want you,' he whispered hoarsely as his mouth moved against her ear, nuzzling, moving down her neck, blazing a trail of feather-light kisses which seared her skin. 'I want you.'

His mouth moved on, reached a hollow in her neck, moved round to an ear before retracing its path. And,

while his mouth explored her neck, her mouth, her face,
his hands slid down her body, easily disposing of the
robe, until only the flimsy lace lay between his hands
and her eager flesh. Even this was too much of a barrier
and Luke pushed the material off her shoulders, tugging
it the length of her body until Celina lay quite naked on
the bed. He paused again, his eyes probing every inch,
and she lay still, knowing from the tender smile that
played about his lips that her body pleased him. One
hand caressed her, traced the outline of her breasts, her
waist, her hips, her thighs, while his eyes locked with
hers. She returned his gaze with steady, smouldering eyes,
content to wait, more than content to allow his hands
to roam, his fingers to explore the secret, sacred parts
of her.

She ran her tongue over dry lips and Luke smiled
again, dipping his head, tracing the outline of her mouth
with his tongue, moistening, nuzzling, sending her half
crazy with desire. Her body flamed as he took pos-
session of her mouth, as his hands stroked and kneaded,
glided and caressed, triggering responses Celina hadn't
known existed.

The kisses went on and on, intoxicatingly heady, and
then Luke's lips began their journey down her body,
reaching her breasts, circling them with kisses slow and
languorous, tantalising almost, before homing in on each
straining, shockingly sensitive pink tip.

Celina moaned, moving her body to meet his hands,
his lips, wanting it never to end, Luke's mouth and
tongue sliding over her skin, driving her to distraction.
He followed the outline of each leg, down one, up the
other, kneeling beside her on the bed, an errant lock of
hair falling over one eye, giving him a vulnerable,
loveable, boyish appearance, and Celina's eyes were
drawn to the lightly tanned skin, the rippling muscles,
the powerful thighs with their covering of golden hair
so fine that she reached out a hand to stroke him.

Luke moaned then, moving his body even closer, burying his face in her hair, and Celina felt the strength of him, her heart soaring as she realised that this man wanted her every bit as much as she wanted him.

His mouth became more urgent, bruising, but the sensation was exquisite and Celina could only part her lips, return the pressure, taste his tongue with her own. And all the time his hands were ranging her body, stroking, caressing, kneading, giving pleasure wherever they made contact with her skin.

Celina writhed uncontrollably, a mass of quivering nerve-ends, and still Luke's mouth explored hers, still the fingers probed, taking her higher and higher until she was almost ready to explode. And yet every time she thought he had lifted her to the very heights of passion his fingers found another secret part, triggered off another soaring explosion, lifting her to fever-pitch.

She opened her eyes, tracing the contours of his face, loving the expression in his smoky blue eyes, and loving even more the weight of him, the unbelievable sensation of his body against hers. He paused, an exquisite, tantalising, breathtaking moment, before smiling a tender smile, sensing she was ready, his eyes fastened on hers, locking with hers as they reached the moment of entry.

Confusion. Luke's movements faltered, a whole host of emotions flitting across his face as he met with a resistance he hadn't expected: puzzlement, dawning recognition, doubt, disbelief, horror. He tried to draw back as Celina's instincts came into play. Arching her back, she urged herself forwards, re-kindling his impetus, and Luke's body became her body as the fireworks exploded in a glorious, earth-shattering, mind-blowing conclusion.

They lay still on the bed, arms and legs entwined, and the only sound was the steady beat of each heart as their breathing returned to normal and they slept.

* * *

The bed was empty when she woke, and but for the crumpled sheets she might have believed that she had dreamt it. And yet the whole night was so firmly impressed upon her mind that it couldn't have been a dream. Eight hours later her body still tingled from Luke's kisses and touch. And now he was gone. She didn't know what to think. She should have been the happiest woman in the world. Had Luke's tousled blond head been beside her on the pillow she would have been. As it was, his absence unnerved her, casting a shadow, taking on looming proportions which sent a chill to the very core of her.

It had been everything she had ever hoped for and more, much more, and Luke hadn't been short-changed, she was sure of that in her innocence. And she loved him. Perhaps now he would know just how much she loved him. Her body couldn't lie, and the message must have been clear enough.

The door opened, slowly, cautiously, and Luke's head appeared around the jamb. He smiled gravely when he saw she was awake.

'Good morning, sleepy-head,' he said, carrying a cup of tea across the room and placing it on the bedside table.

Celina wriggled herself into a sitting position, suddenly shy under his gaze, and she hugged the sheet to her body as Luke's eyes swept over her.

He sat down on the side of the bed, waiting until Celina had taken a few sips of her tea. 'Why didn't you tell me?' he asked gently.

Celina smiled tremulously. 'Would you have believed me?'

Luke shook his head. 'Probably not,' he agreed, and then they both fell silent.

Celina sipped her tea, sensing he had something to say, content to bide her time. She drained the cup and replaced it. He wasn't happy. The bubble of joy popped inside her head. 'What's wrong, Luke?' she asked, voice not quite steady.

He turned his head, eyes bleak, full of conflict, and the blood began to freeze in her veins. 'I'm sorry,' he said simply, taking hold of her shoulders. Celina tried to tear her gaze away, not believing the words, not believing the truth reflected in his eyes, and yet horribly afraid that she'd be forced to. 'It shouldn't have happened,' Luke told her quietly, insistently. 'I shouldn't have let it happen. It won't happen again, I promise you.'

'But we're married,' Celina protested, wanting to throw herself against his chest, feel his arms about her body as he held her close.

Cruel fingers dug into her shoulders, keeping them apart. 'It's a piece of paper, Celina, an agreement, an arrangement. It doesn't entitle me to the run of the bedroom.'

'But it's my marriage as well,' she pointed out. 'I wanted you too.'

'Oh, yes.' He smiled bitterly. 'I can be pretty persuasive when the occasion demands. But it doesn't alter a thing. It's a paper marriage for paper people. We both had reasons, but let's not kid ourselves; love never entered into it, and the last thing either of us needs just now is emotional complications. It won't happen again, Celina,' he repeated. 'I won't let it.'

He stood up, holding her gaze for a long, long moment before crossing to the door, closing it quietly, firmly behind him, and Celina sat frozen on the bed, completely alone, more alone than she had ever been, and, as her unseeing eyes continued to stare at the spot where a moment earlier Luke had been standing, convulsive sobs rose in her throat, racking her body as the tears poured unchecked, stingingly down her cheeks.

CHAPTER EIGHT

'Is something bothering you?'

Celina paused, mascara-brush halfway to her lashes, catching Luke's eye in the mirror. He was standing in the doorway, a quizzical expression on his face, and as Celina looked up he moved across to stand behind her, placing his hands lightly on her shoulders, holding her gaze in the glass.

She felt herself blushing, his presence in her bedroom unusual, unnerving, every bit as unnerving as the fingers gently massaging her taut flesh, and the mascara bottle slipped from her fingers, landing with a clatter on the dressing-table, making her jump.

'What's wrong, Celina?' he asked again.

'Nothing. Nothing at all,' she lied. 'Why should there be?'

'You're being evasive,' Luke replied gravely.

'Am I?' She gave a nervous little laugh, finding the contact of his fingers on her bare skin almost more than she could stand.

'You know you are.'

There was a long, uneasy pause while Celina fumbled with her make-up bag, unconsciously opening and shutting the clasp.

'If I ask a question, a personal question, will you give me an honest answer?' Luke enquired solemnly.

'I'll try,' Celina told him, her heart beginning to thump uncomfortably in her breast.

Luke spun her round to face him, his eyes dark, searching, enquiring. 'Is it me?' he asked. 'Something I've said? Something I've done?'

There was another loaded pause and Celina held her breath, knowing full well what was running through his mind, her own bitter-sweet memories of the night so deeply engraved that she could recall in perfect detail every kiss, every touch, every single nuance of expression.

'Celina——'

'No, Luke,' she interrupted. 'I know what you're thinking and you're wrong. Forget that. It wasn't your fault. It wasn't anybody's fault and it didn't upset me. I promise you.'

'You're sure?'

Oh, yes, I'm sure, Celina mocked silently. That came later, waking up, finding you gone, facing up to reality. She swallowed her pain, nodding across reassuringly. 'I'm sure.'

Luke smiled fleetingly. 'I'm glad. I thought— I *hoped* I hadn't hurt you, but you've seemed so unhappy these past few weeks. What is it, Celina? Can't you tell me?'

Celina shook her head, closing her eyes, blocking him out. How could she even begin? There was too much bottled up inside her now. Her father, Luke, the spectre of Maressa. Everything had been fine, had been going so well, their lives beginning to take on a recognisable shape, when overnight, it seemed, everything had altered. Luke had been so busy, preoccupied, working long hours, leaving her alone with time to think, time to brood, time to wonder, and with Maressa in the background... The threads of doubt were there, biding their time, snaking their way in at unguarded moments. And, even without Maressa, there were the worries about her father.

'Why can't we talk?' Luke asked. 'Why don't we talk any more? You're putting up barriers, shutting me out.'

'I'm not shutting you out, Luke,' Celina told him, turning back to her make-up, gathering up the tubes and pots and putting them back in the hold-all.

'Then why aren't we talking any more?' he demanded urgently.

'Perhaps we've nothing to say,' Celina countered over-brightly.

Luke tucked a hand under her chin, lifting her head, forcing her to look at him. 'You don't believe that and neither do I. You're brooding. There's something on your mind. I may be wrong but I don't think it's me or you or the state of our marriage. I could handle that. It would be the easiest thing in the world. But it isn't. There's something else. Why can't you tell me?'

'I'm surprised you're even interested,' Celina flung out, his sudden perception catching her off guard.

'Of course I'm interested. You're my wife. What do you take me for, for goodness' sake? I'm not a monster, Celina. I care.'

'Do you?' Celina's mouth twisted. Yes, he probably did, too, in a way, but he'd never understand. They came from different worlds. He was a hard-headed business-man, highly motivated and ruthlessly determined to have his own way. People, personality and emotion would never form part of his calculations. She could tell him about her father, and then what? He'd be livid for a start, Celina having lied and deliberately misled him. He could end it all then, their sham of a marriage, but that blow had to come sooner or later in any case. No, it wasn't that. She'd steeled herself for that. It was her father himself she was protecting. He'd suffered so much already, all the scorn and condemnation, the mass of bad publicity crucifying, pushing him over the edge. Everyone had turned against him, friends and family alike, feeding his guilt, the weight of guilt Celina had fought so hard to lift. If she could pay off the smaller investors, the ones hit most badly by the company's col-lapse, she'd actually stand a chance, the doctors had told her after his stroke. It was a mammoth task, on top of the nursing-home fees an almost impossible one, and yet she'd done so much because she loved him. She loved Luke too, now. How could she live with the knowledge that the most important man in her life could have no respect for her father? While Luke was kept in ignorance it was easier to accept. It might be contempt and condemnation, the response Celina had been conditioned to expect, or it might be something milder—pity, perhaps, or indifference. But however Luke reacted she'd be hurt, very hurt, and she wasn't ready yet to face that pain.

'I care,' Luke repeated, dragging her thoughts back to their conversation. 'I care about you. You're unhappy. I can't stand by and watch you like this.'

'You're all heart, aren't you, Luke?' Celina found herself goading, hitting out, wanting to hurt. 'You'll have me weeping buckets next.'

Luke's mouth twisted into an angry line, but the expression vanished just as quickly. 'You're overwrought,' he said mildly. 'You're working too hard, letting things get to you. Why not take a few days off? Come with me to Paris on Thursday.' He smiled suddenly, his face lighting up. 'Yes, why not?' he urged. 'It's a good idea, Celina, a few days away. I won't be working all the time. Come with me.'

'I can't just drop everything and go, Luke. I work for a living, remember?'

'But you don't have to. There's no earthly reason why you should.'

'Except that I want to.'

'There's no answer to that one, is there?'

'I enjoy my job,' Celina explained defensively.

'Well, something's making you unhappy. If it isn't the job, that only leaves me, doesn't it?'

'No.'

'Yes.'

'You wouldn't understand.'

'You won't give me the chance to. Damn it all, Celina, you're not being fair.'

'Why? Because I refuse to confide in you? Because I won't give up my job? Because I retain my independence, keep my thoughts to myself? You don't own me lock, stock and barrel, Luke. I'm not some inanimate object you can keep hidden away and bring out to dust semi-occasionally. I'm flesh and blood, a living being with a mind of my own. I have needs and feelings. When I'm happy I laugh, and when I'm hurt I cry.'

'No, you don't. You won't allow yourself to. It's a weakness, in your eyes, part of your strong northern upbringing.'

'And what would you know about it?' she demanded bitterly.

'I know a lot more than you'd imagine, Celina,' Luke replied gently.

He knows! she thought, a strange tremor running through her. He knows! She realised she was twisting her hands together in her lap and she forced herself to relax. Luke was watching her carefully, his blue eyes cloudy with concern. He can't know, she decided, jumping up, turning away from him, checking her handbag for hairbrush, tissues, purse. He senses something but that's all. He couldn't possibly know the truth. The idea was ridiculous. How could he know?

She picked up her jacket. 'I'm ready,' she said, falsely cheerful, slipping it over her shoulders. 'If we don't leave soon we're going to miss the start of the performance.'

He seemed about to speak, shook his head slightly, and then moved to the door, waiting for Celina to precede him through it. As she drew level he put out a hand, touching her arm, halting her. 'I know you don't have a very high opinion of me,' he said huskily, 'but if you can bring yourself to trust me, Celina, I won't let you down. I promise I won't let you down.'

Celina gulped, swallowing the lump in her throat, blinking back the tears. She nodded, not trusting herself to speak.

The doorbell rang. Celina was surprised. With Luke away she wasn't expecting visitors. She put down her book. Luke had been gone over forty-eight hours and still she couldn't settle. She had spent the first night wandering about the apartment, fingering the ornaments, dusting away imaginary specks of dust. She had started a new book, the latest Mary Wesley, but she'd soon put it down, switching on the TV, half watching a sit-com that seemed anything but funny, turning that off and deciding to listen to some music instead. Even Bryan Ferry couldn't soothe her, and she had finally gone to bed, tossing and turning for most of the night, waking far too early but unable to drop off again.

Friday had been little better. Anita had suggested a night out and Celina had almost been tempted, but Luke would ring, she was sure of it, and she didn't want to miss it. Anita had smiled very knowingly at the subsequent refusal.

Following their intense conversation, Celina had forced herself out of her depression. It wasn't fair on Luke, wallowing in gloomy thoughts, making herself miserable, worrying him, and the last few days had seen them slip back into something more like their earlier relationship. It wasn't perfect by any means, but it was an improvement, and at least it was progress.

The buzzer went again. 'OK, OK, I'm coming. Yes?' She spoke into the intercom.

'Celina, my love, do let me in. It's freezing down here.'

'Danny! What on earth——?' She punched out the code, giving him access to their lift, and then crossed the hall to meet him.

'Surprise, surprise!' Danny burst out as the lift doors swung open. 'I just knew you'd be brooding, so here I am, a knight in shining armour to the rescue.' Before she could stop him he'd gathered her into his arms, planting a huge kiss firmly on her mouth.

'Danny!' Celina protested, pushing herself away.

'It's all right, sister-in-law. I have the picture. You're Luke's property now. Pity, we could have had some fun.'

'Danny!' Celina objected again, her tone a little bit sharper. 'If this is the sort of mood you're in I think you'd better leave.'

'And waste a perfectly good bottle of bubbly? All right, Celina, I'll be good, I promise.' He crossed his heart in the age-old gesture of childhood.

'Empty words, Danny. I'd almost forgotten you had the gift of the gab and could charm the leaves from the trees without effort.'

She followed him into the kitchen, reaching for the glasses, looking on as he eased the cork gently out of the bottle. Champagne wasn't her favourite drink and she wasn't sure Danny should even be here with Luke away, but half an hour wouldn't hurt and it would seem churlish turning him away after he'd made the effort.

It was the first time she'd seen him since before her wedding. The rift between the brothers had more or less healed, Celina gathered from the odd remark Luke had let fall. Danny had sent a wedding gift, some beautiful Waterford crystal, and Celina had sent a note of thanks, following it up with a phone call. She was relieved that contact had been re-established, but, taking her cue from Luke, had made no further effort to draw Danny into their newly arranged lives.

She still wondered occasionally why he'd let her down, but as time went on it seemed less and less important, and, besides, Luke had made no secret of his own involvement. Interference would have been Celina's description of Luke's manipulations but it was water under the bridge now, she supposed.

Danny raised the champagne flute. 'Here's to wedded bliss,' he toasted. 'To you and Luke, and the patter of tiny feet.'

Celina's cheeks flamed. 'Dan-ny!' she exclaimed one more time, her tone perceptibly hardening. 'I thought you'd promised to behave.'

But Danny merely grinned good-naturedly, not a bit put out.

He hadn't changed much, she decided as the night went on and he made no effort to take himself off. She sipped her wine in a lull between the bouts of laughter, unconsciously comparing him to Luke and reaching the conclusion that fate had known best when the brothers had changed places in her life. Danny was fun, but how *young* he seemed, full of madcap ideas and harebrained plans for the future.

True, Danny could make her laugh, but only Luke could give her what she needed. She felt a stab of pain and her lips twisted into a bitter line. Luke couldn't give her what she needed. That's why it hurt so much, loving him, aching for him, knowing that he would never love her. Danny caught the grimace.

'Something wrong?' he asked, placing his glass on the table and leaning forward, his brow creased with concern.

'A slight twinge of indigestion,' Celina lied. 'I ate too much at tea. Mrs Wilson had left my favourite, Lancashire hotpot, and I'm afraid to say I didn't leave a morsel.'

'Are you sure?' Danny queried, his expression for once perfectly serious.

Celina raised an eyebrow. 'About what I ate? Oh, yes, I think so,' she replied with assumed flippancy.

Danny smiled also. 'That isn't what I meant, and well you know it,' he chided mildly, but he let the subject drop, raising it again an hour later.

He'd stood up to leave, stretching his long limbs before reaching for his jacket carelessly flung on the back of the settee. He paused, and Celina waited for him to speak, sensing he had something on his mind.

'You can tell me to mind my own business, Celina, but there is something bothering you, isn't there? Luke?'

'Not really.'

'Not really, which, roughly translated, probably means yes. Am I right, or am I right?'

'You're an idiot, Danny, do you know?'

'So I've been told. And stop changing the subject. I may be a clown but I have my share of intuition. Come on, tell Danny-boy. Spill the beans, or whatever it is you're bottling up inside.'

'It's nothing. Honestly.'

'Sure?'

'I'm sure.'

'Hm. Well, tell me something, then.'

Celina smiled. 'If I can.'

'Do you love him, Celina, really love him?'

'Yes, Danny, very much.'

He brightened up at once. 'I'm glad. I've been worried about you, but I should have known you'd be all right. After all, Luke went to great lengths to get you for himself.'

'After *you* stood me up,' she couldn't resist needling.

'Me?' Danny laughed, throwing back his head, filling the room with a warm, vibrant sound.

'Did I say something funny?' Celina asked, the merest hint of asperity in her tone.

'You bet you did.'

'Going to let me in on the joke?' she demanded.

Danny shook his head. 'Ask Luke.'

'I'm asking you.'

'Oh, Celina, you're priceless, you really are. I didn't stand you up.'

'No?'

'No. How could you think such thoughts of me, *me*, who loved you to distraction, worshipped the ground you walked on, kissed the——'

'Cut it out, Danny, I'm serious.'

'You're no fun any more. It's plain to see the man's a sobering influence, killing your sense of humour, shrivelling—— '

'Quit stalling, Danny. I'm waiting, Danny, and I'm running out of patience—fast.' She glared at him, her face as thunderous as she could make it in the circumstances. 'Now, are you going to tell me or shall I fetch a long and exceedingly sharp knife from the kitchen and hold it to your throat?'

'You wouldn't, woman.'

'Wouldn't I?'

'Ah, yes, I believe she would, at that,' he told no one in particular.

Celina folded her arms. 'Danny!'

'Yes, my love?'

'I'm not your love. I never was and never shall be. Now, for the last time, why didn't you turn up for the wedding?'

'I was—er—otherwise engaged,' he told her, looking sheepish.

'Yes?'

'Yes. That's it. Dead simple.'

'Not to me. I was hurt. Not a word, not a hint, nothing. Just an absent bridegroom. Why, Danny, why?'

'You really want to know?'

'I'm just mildly curious,' Celina replied with heavy sarcasm.

'Didn't Luke tell you?'

'You know he didn't.'

'He locked me in the bathroom.'

Celina looked on, speechless, his words going in but barely registering. For a full thirty seconds she didn't react at all. Danny's face was a picture, a comic mix of humour and embarrassment and, as Celina continued to stare open-mouthed, the bubbles of fun inside her began to pop. She laughed outright.

'You're joking,' she spluttered through the tears of laughter. 'Aren't you?'

Danny shook his head, his expression glum. 'I fail to see what's so funny,' he protested, looking hurt.

'Now who's lost his sense of humour?' she chided lightly.

'It wasn't funny, Celina.'

'No, Danny.'

'It still isn't funny, Celina.'

'No, Danny.'

Their eyes met and the laughter bubbled up again, Danny's features softening, despite himself.

'Oh, Danny,' Celina gasped, the tears rolling down her cheeks. 'And you tell me I'm priceless.'

'Somebody sounds happy.'

'Luke!' Celina's eyes widened, the pupils narrowing to tiny pinpricks of surprise. For a moment she froze, and then the blood rushed to her cheeks, triggering an instinctive reaction. She launched herself across the space between them, flinging herself into his embrace. Luke's eyebrows rose but his arms came round, hugging her close, and Celina raised her face, not giving herself time to think, her lips parting in silent invitation of his kiss. Luke dipped his head, his mouth meeting hers, and inside Celina currents of excitement began to ripple and swirl, gathering force, travelling the length of her, coursing through her veins, setting her on fire.

'And to think you've hardly had time to miss me,' Luke teased, whispering into her ear as the kiss came to an end and his mouth brushed her cheek.

Celina's blush deepened. Having got over her initial surprise, she found herself suddenly shy and awkward, and made to move away. Luke caught the movement.

His hand closed around hers, drawing her back to his side.

'So Danny's been keeping you company, has he?' he asked with a smile.

'I was just going, brother,' Danny put in, heading for the door.

'You don't have to go yet, surely? Come and have a drink. I've brought some cognac—your favourite.'

'Another time,' Danny demurred. 'I was on my way out, and, in any case, I have the distinct impression I've just turned green and hairy.'

'You've what?' Luke asked, for once nonplussed.

Celina giggled nervously. 'He doesn't like playing gooseberry,' she explained.

'It's never bothered him in the past,' Luke commented, shrugging himself out of his coat.

'Well, it's bothering him now,' Danny said. 'I know when I'm not needed. Thanks for the invitation, but I'll take a rain check on the drink.'

And then they were alone.

'Had a good trip?' Celina asked when Luke had changed and rejoined her in the lounge. She was curled up in an armchair, legs tucked underneath her body, arms hugging her knees, suddenly very, very nervous.

'So-so,' Luke replied.

'Why didn't you let me know you were catching an earlier plane? I could have come out to meet you,' she added, watching as he poured himself a drink, long, tapering fingers curled around the bottle.

'I didn't know,' Luke told her. 'Spur of the moment decision, I suppose. I'd just about wrapped everything up and was booked on a plane for tomorrow when I changed my mind, decided to come tonight. I was going to ring but then I thought I'd surprise you. Brandy?' he added, darting her a strange look.

'Please. Just a small one. I've already had some champagne.'

'So I've noticed. It was good of Danny to call. Un-usually thoughtful, in fact.'

'You don't mind?'

A single eyebrow arched. 'Why should I mind?' he asked mildly. 'Danny's my brother, you're my wife. If you can't spend an evening in each other's company, then heaven help us all. Besides,' he darted her another piercing glance, 'he's obviously good for you.'

'And what's that supposed to mean?' Celina asked, her colour rising.

'It's weeks since I heard you laugh, really laugh, and there's some colour in your cheeks for once. Danny must have the magic ingredient. I must ask him how he does it. Unless,' he paused, swirling the golden liquid round and round the brandy goblet, 'unless Danny *is* the magic ingredient.'

'That's a stupid comment,' Celina snapped, catching his meaning at once.

'Is it? I'm not so sure. You never did get to choose between us, did you, Celina? I wonder.'

'I married you,' she pointed out, not liking one bit the direction the conversation was taking.

'Hobson's choice. You'd never have married me if Danny had turned up. You know it, I know it, why not be honest and admit it?'

'But Danny didn't turn up, did he, Luke? He couldn't. You'd made certain of that.'

'Ah. So he told you? I should have expected that.'

'Is that all you have to say?' she demanded, bristling visibly.

'What do you expect me to say? That I'm sorry?' he retorted. 'No, Celina, I'm not sorry. I've never for a moment regretted what I did.'

'No. You wouldn't. You're much too arrogant to waste time on regrets. Why did you do it, Luke?'

'Do what? Marry you? Stop you marrying Danny? I had my reasons.'

'I'll bet you did,' she replied with icy venom, eyes flashing dangerously across at him. 'And is that what you told Danny? You must have been so sure of yourself. After all, you can hardly keep a grown man locked up for long without arousing suspicion. You sent him away, Luke. Not as early as you led people to believe, but you must have been very persuasive, keeping him away from me once you did release him. How did you manage that? Dangled another carrot, did you?'

'Not exactly.'

'Not exactly?' Celina's voice rose. 'And what's that supposed to mean? And, before you conjure up another of your plausible explanations, just let me remind you: I *know* Danny. He let me down. He had his arm twisted, I'm sure of it.'

Luke shrugged. 'Danny's very skilled at creating the wrong impression, Celina. He might have wanted to marry you, but it wasn't for love, even you've admitted that. And as for reasons, let's just say that Danny listened to common sense for once. We made a bargain. He was to make no effort to contact you at all for six weeks, and if, on his return, you were both intent on going ahead with the marriage then fine, I'd withdraw my objections.'

'Oh, very noble,' Celina sneered. 'What's it like playing God, Luke? Gives you a kick, does it, a cheap thrill?'

'It wasn't like that, Celina.'

'Come off it. You can't fool me. You didn't give a damn, not for Danny, not for me. You did what you wanted for your own twisted reasons. And once Danny was safely out of the way you made sure he wouldn't marry me. Very clever, Luke, very clever indeed. Proud of yourself?'

'You didn't *have* to marry me, Celina,' he pointed out logically.

'I didn't *have* to do anything, but I did, didn't I?'

'So what's the problem?'

'You're the problem,' she spat. 'Playing God, making all the decisions, planning my every move for me. You could have ruined my life.'

'And did I?'

'Yes! No! I don't know. I don't know,' she repeated, her anger dying as quickly as it had flared, and then, fingers slowly unclenching in her lap, 'No,' she admitted. 'Danny's fun, but it would have been a mistake. I can see that now.'

'And was I a mistake too?' Luke asked quietly, so quietly that Celina had to strain to catch the words. 'Was I, Celina?'

She dropped her eyes.

'*Was* I, Celina?' he persisted. '*Was* I?'

Celina swallowed hard. 'I—I—don't know,' she stammered, taking refuge in the lie, hating herself.

'Look at me,' he commanded.

She raised her head slowly, forcing herself to meet his gaze, reading nothing in the tight set of his lips, the dark and hooded eyes. He watched her for a long, long moment while Celina froze, conscious that she'd let him down, hurt him, hurt herself more.

Picking up his glass, he drained the contents in one. 'I'm going to bed,' he said wearily, standing up, not even glancing in her direction. 'It's been a long day. Goodnight.'

Celina sat on for another ten minutes, hardly moving, hardly breathing. She really had let him down, and the knowledge was like a poison, eating away at her. She sipped the last of her brandy, her thoughts racing, the germ of an idea beginning to take shape. Finally she nodded. She'd have to risk a rebuff but it was worth the gamble. She'd do it.

The light underneath Luke's door went out as she drew level. Even better. The darkness made it easier, would stop him from seeing her face, would mask her feelings if it all went wrong.

'Celina?' he asked as she tiptoed naked across the deep pile of the carpet and slipped in beside him.

'Expecting someone else?' she quipped, running her hand across his chest, tangling her fingers in the mass of curls that covered it.

'You're playing with fire, Celina,' he warned tersely, wrapping iron fingers round her wrist, halting her.

'Frightened you'll get burnt, Luke?' she goaded gently, nervously, voice not quite steady.

'You, lady, are a she-devil. In the old days they'd have drowned you as a witch.'

'I might have floated, Luke,' Celina pointed out logically and, sensing her advantage, wriggled closer, bringing her body into contact with his.

'Not a hope in hell,' he groaned, burying his face in her hair and drawing her even closer. 'Are you sure you know what you're doing?' he asked, mouth nuzzling her ear, lips beginning to trace the outline of her jaw.

'No, Luke,' Celina answered with more than a hint of laughter as his hands began to roam her body, hesitantly at first and then more confidently as he met with her response. 'But I'm sure as hell going to enjoy finding out!'

CHAPTER NINE

'TONY DANVERS dropped into the office yesterday,' Luke mentioned a couple of days later over breakfast. 'He and Adèle are free Saturday. Feel up to entertaining in for a change?'

'How much entertaining?' Celina asked, reaching for the marmalade. So far when they'd wined and dined Luke's clients they'd eaten out at one of their favourite restaurants, usually following on from a show, and Celina had enjoyed every moment. Entertaining at home, though, was a whole new step, and Celina recognised that it was a subtle vote of confidence from Luke, both in her ability to organise and carry it off, and in their changed relationship.

After her night of daring she hadn't known what to expect, but waking up the following morning still firmly cocooned in Luke's arms had sent another thrill of pleasure pulsing through her. She had lain perfectly still, watching his sleeping face, not wanting to break the spell, dreading the possible outcome. But Luke had finally wakened and smiled his lazy smile, and Celina had known, even before his hands began to range her body, that it was going to be all right.

'Just a small dinner party,' Luke now explained, pouring out a second cup of coffee. 'Nothing too formal, six or eight altogether.'

Celina swallowed a smile. 'Nothing too formal' probably meant four courses at least, but that was nothing to worry about. She wouldn't be doing the cooking; nor would the invaluable Mrs Wilson. A first-class firm of caterers would take the sting out of the entire occasion, leaving Celina with little to do but supervise and ensure that everyone was made to feel at ease.

In the event it was rather a mixed evening. Celina had been surprised when the six or eight guests had grown to eight or ten, and was even more amazed when it had turned out that Danny and a girlfriend would make it twelve. She was glad. It meant the rift between the brothers had definitely healed, although, once Saturday evening itself arrived, there were moments when she suspected it must have widened.

Anita and Zac were the first to arrive, closely followed by the Danvers. They were a lovely couple, in their forties, Celina would guess, and from Vancouver. They were so obviously pleased to be there that Celina's last-minute attack of nerves vanished at once. Everything would be fine, she told herself, sipping a diluted vodka and tonic, and, by the time the other guests arrived, was feeling quietly confident.

With just Danny and his partner still to come, Celina slipped away for a moment, double-checking the seating plan and the table layout. There was no real need, she acknowledged, pausing on the threshold and running a critical eye over the sparkling silver and the gleaming crystal. Everything was perfect, and she was smiling to herself as she returned to the drawing-room.

Celina walked in through one door as Danny and a tall, willowy and extremely beautiful woman walked in through another. Celina didn't quite know why, but her feeling of well-being disappeared at once. Automatically she moved to Luke's side as he stepped forward to make the introductions.

'Maressa Forbes,' he said smoothly, blandly. 'Glad you could come.'

She should have guessed then, Celina realised later, having intercepted the withering glance Luke shot at Danny. Danny had raised his head, meeting Luke's gaze, his expression half sheepish, half defiant. All the clues were there and yet still she ignored the warning bells that were ringing in her ears.

They were halfway through the main course when the truth hit her. Choking on a piece of meat and coughing with embarrassment, Celina's blush deepened as everyone looked up. With a muttered apology she ran from the room, locking herself in the bathroom. The coughing fit passed. She sat on the edge of the bath, sipping a glass of water, taking deep, even breaths in an effort to bring her emotions under control. She stared at her reflection in the mirror on the wall. Twin spots of colour dominated the centre of her otherwise pale cheeks, and the eyes that looked back at her were suddenly very, very frightened.

There was a low knock at the door. 'Celina?' Luke's voice drifted through. 'Are you all right?'

'Just coming,' she replied, forcing some enthusiasm into her tone. She straightened her spine as she opened the door.

Luke stood there, a frown of concern furrowing his brow. 'All right?' he enquired, relaxing as he took her hands in his.

Celina nodded.

'Good girl.' He leaned forward, planting a light kiss on her forehead. 'Let's go back in. Your dinner will be getting cold.'

That's not all that's getting cold, Celina thought as they re-entered the dining-room and she found her gaze instinctively drawn to the cool brown eyes of Danny's partner. Luke's former mistress smiled knowingly across and the icy finger tightened its grip on Celina's heart. She *should* have known, and yet was it so surprising that she hadn't?

The two women had never met, Maressa having upped and married the wealthy Jeremy Forbes at about the time Celina had started seeing Danny. She'd been a name from the past, a shadow hovering in the background, but was now, suddenly, disturbingly, a very real threat to the present.

Celina's eyes were drawn to the top of the table, where Luke's blond head was angled towards Maressa on his left, and all the doubts and uncertainties rose up to plague her. Could it *really* have been coincidence that Luke had married Celina just as Maressa's divorce had come through, or was her gut reaction the right one? And, if it was a cold and calculated attempt on Luke's part to pay Maressa back, hadn't the punishment gone far enough? He'd made his point, surely, and in that case Celina was redundant. He didn't need her any more.

Celina shuddered, shutting out the picture that sprang to mind. She swallowed another mouthful of lemon soufflé and reached for her glass. The meal had been superb, though Celina had barely tasted the beautifully prepared food that was placed before her. The evening had gone well so far, the atmosphere convivial and the service so unobtrusive that they could have been in a top-class restaurant in the heart of Paris or any of the world's leading cities. It was something to be thankful for, she supposed, that everyone else seemed to be enjoying it.

The ladies left the men to their cigars, Adèle Danvers issuing a gentle warning to her husband. 'Remember what the doctors say,' she admonished lightly. Then added for everyone's else's benefit, 'I've been telling Tony for years that he's slowly killing himself, but he takes not the slightest bit of notice.'

'Oh, but I do, my dear,' her husband contradicted, face perfectly serious. 'I listen to every word you say, and I fully agree.'

'So why haven't you given it up, then?' Adèle demanded with a small smile of triumph.

'You'd have nothing to nag me about if I did,' he replied as everyone laughed.

Celina led the way to the drawing-room. It wasn't a room they used very often, preferring the lounge, which was smaller, cosier, warmer, but this was ideal for entertaining, easily taking a dozen people and still not seeming crowded.

'Coffee?' Celina asked. 'Or shall we wait for the others?'

'Brandy for me, please.' Maressa sank down on one of the settees, leaning back against the cushions, her long legs stretched out in front of her. Celina wondered how she could possibly breathe. The dress, obviously tailor-made for her, fitted like a second skin, the vivid orange silk seemed moulded to her body, the knee-length skirt emphasising the slender lines of the incredibly long legs. She reminded Celina of a dark-haired version of Jerry Hall, and beside her she felt downright gauche. Her own outfit was a new one, the full, filmy skirt reaching below her calves and swirling round her legs in a cloud of deepest blues and purples with occasional splashes of green. She had shown it to Luke on the day she'd bought it, pleased at his reaction. The colours suited her, he'd told her warmly, and had then casually enquired when she would wear it.

Nervous fingers were drawn to the emerald at her throat. It was a gift from Luke, along with matching earrings, and she'd been touched when he'd handed her the long, slim box just as she'd finished dressing, ridiculously pleased at the trouble he'd taken in choosing something that picked out the green in her dress so perfectly. It probably meant little to Luke, and she'd been careful not to over-react, remembering another piece of jewellery and another occasion.

Maressa's eyes met Celina's. 'Is smoking confined to the gentlemen?' she asked mockingly as Celina handed her a brandy goblet. 'I'm simply dying for a smoke, if you'll excuse the pun. Perhaps I ought to rejoin the boys.'

'Not at all,' Celina replied. 'I'll find you an ashtray.'

The conversation could have been stilted but thankfully Adèle and Anita took the lead, keeping up a light chatter which soon included everyone—except Maressa. She seemed more than content to sit back, taking little part, chipping in with a comment every now and again, although, Celina noticed with malicious delight, she did liven up considerably once 'the boys' came back in.

In the meantime, Adèle was talking. 'What a beautiful apartment,' she told Celina. 'You don't know how lucky you are living in London. We move around such a lot that there's no one place we call home. One of these days I'm going to insist we settle down, and when we do I want something just like this.'

'Thank you.' Celina smiled. 'I think it's lovely, too, but Luke's decided it's not quite big enough now. We're house-hunting, so it's only a matter of time before we move.'

'How exciting. Have you anywhere in mind?'

'Not really. We've short-listed a few but we haven't actually been out to look. We've both been so busy lately that there just hasn't been time when we're both free.'

'Don't tell me you're still working,' Maressa interjected. 'How quaint.'

How vulgar, she might have added, the meaning coming across crystal-clear to Celina.

'On the contrary,' Adèle protested with a smile, 'how modern; such a good idea, too, retaining some independence.'

Maressa simply shrugged her elegant shoulders and went back to her brandy.

The atmosphere lifted when Luke and the others rejoined them, the background music soon drowned out by the lively conversation, and for once Danny's jokes were welcome relief. They kept Celina permanently doubled up, and at least while she was laughing her mind wasn't straying along painful pathways.

The subject inevitably turned to business. Tony Danvers was an avid collector of twentieth-century art deco covers, original hand-bound books valued for their leather and gold bindings rather than their content. Luke had managed to track down a much sought-after Paul Bonet which Tony was keen to add to his collection.

'I don't understand what all the fuss is about,' Adèle interrupted Tony's animated description. 'Surely books are meant to be read, not stuck in some display-case, gathering dust?'

'Celina's probably better qualified to answer that than I am,' Tony demurred good-humouredly. 'She's a librarian.'

'Oh! Another book-enthusiast. In that case you'll know what people usually do with the books they borrow, won't you, Celina?'

Celina had to smile. 'You'd be surprised,' she admitted. 'There's a whole range of uses for library books, judging from the state some of them come back in. Propping open doors, holding up furniture, hot-pan stands. You name it, people have probably done it.'

Tony Danvers spread his hands expansively. 'You see,' he explained to his wife, 'I'm not the only one with crazy ideas.'

'The difference is yours are such *expensive* crazy ideas,' Adèle reproved mock-severely. 'Still, I shall remind you of that next week when we fly out to Paris and I make a bee-line for the dress shops.'

'I just love Paris,' Maressa interjected, drawing attention back to herself. Celina swallowed a smile.

'I've never been,' Adèle admitted, 'so I'm really excited. I've always wanted a French wardrobe so I'm going to make the most of it, too. I might never get the chance again.'

'The boutiques are superb,' Maressa agreed. 'I buy most of my clothes there. I must make five or six visits a year.'

'If I lived in London I'd do the same. That's a beautiful creation,' Adèle remarked, indicating Maressa's vivid orange outfit. 'It's a Laroche, isn't it? I recognise the colour.'

Maressa smiled, and Celina was reminded of a sleek cat purring with pleasure. 'Yes it is,' she admitted. 'One of the latest. I picked it up only last week, didn't I, Luke?'

There was a loaded pause. Celina's eyes flew to Luke's, catching his reaction for a fraction of a second, the shutters coming down as their eyes met, cutting him off, shielding him. He returned her gaze unblinkingly, his face impassive, unperturbed.

The chatter started up again, too loud, too quickly, too many people anxious to cover the social gaffe. Accidental? Celina doubted it. Maressa had been out to cause trouble and now she'd succeeded. Celina's cheeks ached from the effort of seeming unconcerned, the painted smile never for a moment slipping. Her eyes stung with unshed tears and inside her head she was talking to herself.

Maressa had wanted to embarrass her, she reasoned. The comment had been deliberate, premeditated, calculated to cause pain. Luke had not been in Paris with Maressa. He couldn't, he wouldn't, she wouldn't let herself believe it. He *couldn't* have gone with Maressa, he simply couldn't. And hadn't he come home early? she reminded herself, clutching at the thought, wanting to believe it. Hardly the actions of a man resuming an affair.

For Celina the evening was ruined. She moved round automatically, supplying drinks, making small talk, laughing at jokes she barely heard. She poured herself a large vodka and tonic and, finding the ice-bucket empty, seized the chance to escape for a while, slipping into the kitchen, taking her time. The caterers had gone, leaving everything pristine. They could have been a figment of her imagination for all the impact they had made, and how she wished that they were, that the whole evening were, that she could wake up in the morning and discover that it was just one long and horrible dream.

Refilling the ice-trays with water, she closed the freezer door as a shiver of premonition ran down her spine. Turning her head, she found herself face to face with Maressa. She was propped up in the doorway, watching Celina, blocking her exit.

'You do know he only married you on the rebound,' Maressa informed her, lips curling in derision. 'On the rebound from me.'

'Really?' Celina retorted coolly, determined not to be drawn.

'Yes, really. And now that I'm back it's only a matter of time before everything's put right. Luke's mine,' Maressa told her, cold brown eyes travelling the length of her, scornful, sneering. 'He's always been mine, and now I've come to claim him.'

'Perhaps he doesn't want you any more,' Celina pointed out, not really believing but not intending either to stand calmly by while Maressa had her say.

Maressa laughed, a harsh, ugly sound, devoid of amusement. 'Don't be so ridiculous,' she derided. 'Of course he wants me. Luke has always wanted me. Oh, I'm sure you've kept him entertained,' she went on, twisting the knife, the cruel words stabbing at Celina, shredding her. 'But that's all it's been, your marriage—a bit of light relief. Even you must see that.'

'Whatever I see, whatever I think is none of your business,' Celina retorted crisply. 'As my marriage is none of your business. But, just for the record, I will tell you this. Luke married me because he wanted to. And in case it had slipped your mind,' she added sweetly, honeyed venom dripping from her tongue, 'he did it *after* you obtained your divorce.'

Celina swept past, head held high, painfully aware that her moment of triumph could be exactly that—fleeting, illusory, self-deceiving. And Maressa was no fool. It wouldn't take her long to work out the other interpretation of Luke's actions. But by then it wouldn't matter. Celina would be alone, hugging her pain, hugging her memories, far away from Maressa's stinging gibes.

The silence was deafening. Celina poured another drink and crossed to the window, drawing back the blinds, staring out into the night.

Normally she loved the view, the lights of the city twinkling like a myriad stars, the illuminated landmarks standing out against the velvet canopy. Tonight her eyes were unseeing; it was the pictures in her mind that occupied her. Maressa in Paris. Luke in Paris. Luke and Maressa in Paris.

She wanted to believe that it was innocent, but Luke hadn't spoken at all since everyone had gone home, and, though the question loomed large between them, Celina didn't want to be the one to bring it up, and yet unless she did she'd never have a moment's peace. And what could she say? If it was true she could hardly object. Theirs wasn't a conventional marriage; Luke had never promised otherwise. He was free to do what he liked, and, if that included sleeping with an old girlfriend, who was Celina to object? The knife plunged deeper. Who indeed?

'Why not get it over and done with?' Luke's voice pierced the uneasy quiet.

Celina spun around, her heart beginning to thump uneasily in her breast. Luke was sitting forward in his chair, jacket and tie discarded, his eyes dark, unreadable. 'Get what over?' she stalled, leaning back against the window, feeling the chill of the glass through the flimsy material of her dress.

'Don't play the innocent, Celina; you know exactly what I mean.'

'Do I? Perhaps I'm not interested, Luke,' she answered coolly.

'You're a liar, Celina, and a bad one at that.'

'Really? How perceptive you are. You'll be telling me my thoughts before I've had time to formulate them next. Just think, you could have a whole new career ahead of you. "Luke Sinclair, clairvoyant. Palm-reading a speciality."'

'Sarcasm doesn't become you,' he replied. 'But, if that's how you want to play it, then fine. That's all right by me. But just remember—you're the one who laid the ground-rules. Don't expect me to play ball when you're eaten up with curiosity and I no longer want to talk.'

'Playing games again, are we?' she asked, her voice hardening. 'What's wrong with plain English, Luke? What's wrong with the truth?'

'You didn't seem particularly interested,' he countered coldly, 'when I brought the subject up.'

'That's because you wrap everything up in a dozen words when one or two would do. You've got a nerve. If you've anything to say, Luke, say it. It's late and I've got a headache.'

'Probably the result of an over-active imagination,' he informed her scathingly.

'And what's that supposed to mean?' she demanded.

'You really are too old to be turning those baby-blue eyes on me like that. You've put Mara and me together in the same city and come up with the magic number. Bingo! Celina's hit the jackpot.'

'Oh, so it's *Mara* now, is it?' Celina rasped. 'Does everyone get to call her that, or just her intimate acquaintances?'

'You're wrong, Celina.'

'Am I?'

'Very, very wrong. Why don't you let me explain?'

'Oh, do go ahead. I'm all ears. I'm sure you'll wrap everything up very nicely, tie up all the loose ends, come up smelling of roses. She just happened to be in Paris, I suppose?'

'Correct.'

'And you just happened to bump into her, I suppose?'

'Also correct.'

'And dinner for two, a spur of the moment invitation, shall I assume?'

'Who said anything about dinner?' he flashed, leaning back, folding his arms, watching her through hooded eyes. 'But yes, Celina, as a matter of fact you're right. You're right on every count so far. You've set the scene perfectly: Act One, Act Two, Act Three, all word-perfect. It's the finale you're going to fluff, though, but why should I bother to refute it? You've made your decision. You're not going to listen to me now. You don't want to.'

'Is that it?' she demanded. 'Is that all you have to say? Don't I get even a hint of a defence?'

'Where's the point?' he asked bitterly. 'I'm already guilty in your eyes. In any case, you can hardly object.'

'And what's that supposed to mean?' Celina asked, eyes widening in alarm.

'You knew what you were getting when you agreed to marry me. I didn't want a conventional marriage, re-member, with mind-numbing scenes such as this? You accepted my terms along with my ring. I thought you could handle my lifestyle. I was wrong. My apologies. I obviously overestimated you. It's something we'll have to discuss some time, and soon. Now, if you'll excuse me.'

'Where are you going?' she barked as he headed for the door, panic rising in her throat, choking her.

He paused on the threshold, his mouth an ugly sneer, his whole expression chillingly contemptuous. 'Don't worry, my dear, I'm not going out to resume where I

left off, however pleasant the thought. I need some fresh
air; the atmosphere in here is stifling. And don't bother
waiting up,' he added derisively. 'I'm a big boy now. I
even have my own key.'

She went to bed. There seemed little point in staying
up. More angry words weren't the answer. The sheets
were cold against her skin, the bed large and empty
without Luke's body. She closed her eyes, willing herself
to sleep, knowing full well she couldn't, not with so much
on her mind. They had come such a long way, and now
this. Her own fault. She'd let her imagination take over,
had lulled herself into a false position. As Luke had
pointed out so cruelly, theirs wasn't a real marriage. Was
it his fault Celina had come to believe that it was?

She thumped her pillow, trying to wriggle down into
a comfortable position. She'd blown it. She hadn't even
cleared the first hurdle. No wonder he despised her. He'd
probably revert to sleeping alone now, and she wouldn't
even be left with the consolation of his body close to
hers in the long hours of the night.

A sob escaped her, but Celina stuffed her fist into her
mouth. She wasn't about to start bawling like a baby,
however tempting the idea. She'd just have to accept the
situation, swallow her pride, apologise. If he ever came
to bed. She checked the time. Forty minutes. Surely he
wasn't going to walk the streets all night? Surely he
wasn't——? But no! She wasn't going back down that
little avenue. She'd done enough damage that way
already. Dry-eyed, she waited, drawing warmth from the
duvet.

She heard a noise and strained her ears. A key in the
lock, a door creaking, a finger of light across the carpet.
Footsteps going into the lounge, footsteps trekking to
the bathroom, the sound of running water. Footsteps
returning, halting—outside her door?

She held her breath. Please, God, she silently prayed,
don't let him go back to his own room. Please.

The door opened. Relief poured over her. 'Luke?' she whispered tentatively as he climbed in beside her.

'Go to sleep, Celina. We can talk in the morning.'

He turned away, his back straight and uncompromising in the gloom. Celina stared at the dark outline and turned over, lying on her side, drawing her knees into her stomach, hugging her misery. The minutes slid by and she could hear the gentle rhythm of his breathing.

The tears welled up and she sniffed, reaching for a tissue. Five minutes later another sob was torn from deep inside. She sat up, trying vainly to control the heaving sobs that racked her.

Arms reached out in the darkness, closing round her shoulders, drawing her down into a warm, safe haven. 'You little fool,' Luke whispered hoarsely. 'I didn't mean to hurt you.'

'I'm s-sorry,' Celina cried, unable to halt the tide of tears. 'I'm s-so sorry.'

'Hush,' he soothed, holding her, rocking her gently backwards and forwards. 'It doesn't matter now. Nothing matters now. Hush, Celina, hush.'

CHAPTER TEN

'PSST. Psst.'

Celina looked up. She was returning books to the shelves and, since it was early morning, had the section to herself. Or so she thought.

'Psst!'

She glanced around. There was no one to be seen, just the shelves of books running the length of the room. She went back to her task, arranging the books on the trolley into alphabetical order. It wasn't a job she normally did but it was something to do, something to keep her busy, too busy to allow wayward thoughts to run unchecked.

Sunday had been a long, long day, Celina refusing to mention Maressa Forbes's name, Luke making no effort to bring the subject up. For Celina it had been a case of two steps forward, one step back, but at least she felt she was moving in the right direction, and she refused to do anything to destroy their fragile peace. Luke would shatter that himself of course, sooner or later, by asking for his freedom. He was teaching Maressa a lesson, Celina was more and more convinced of it. The axe above her head was hanging by a thread, and when it fell she would be devastated, heartbroken, completely alone. But she couldn't face it now, the cold and empty future; couldn't even begin to wonder how she'd cope.

She'd trundled the trolley further down the row, pausing for a moment, head on one side, half convinced there was someone there, when out of the corner of her eye she caught a movement.

She turned her head. A white handkerchief was being fluttered round the edge of the bookcase, waved up and down by some invisible hand. She stood very still, more puzzled than worried, and waited patiently for what would happen next.

'Truce. Truce. Is it safe to come out?' whispered a voice she recognised at once.

'Danny!' she exclaimed, marching down the row to where he was skulking. 'What on earth do you think you're doing?'

'I've come to apologise,' he told her, anxious eyes searching her face. 'I wasn't sure that you'd want to see me.'

'I'm not sure that I want to see you either,' she retorted, clamping her lips together in a thin and angry line. 'In fact, after Saturday I'm surprised you have the gall. Of all the stupid things to do. I'm speechless, Danny; speechless.'

'You really are annoyed, aren't you?' he asked, having the grace to look ashamed.

'Yes,' she told him curtly. 'Annoyed and upset. But it's more than that. Do you know how I really feel, Danny? Do you? I'm disappointed. You let me down—for the second time, Danny. And it hurts.'

Colour flooded into his face. 'I know, Celina. And I am sorry. I didn't mean any harm, not to you. I was showing off, getting at Luke, scoring points, I suppose, turning up with one of his old girlfriends. It simply didn't cross my mind that you'd get hurt as well. It was a stupid thing to do, I can see that now. And I am sorry,' he repeated, eyes silently pleading. 'What else can I say?'

Watching him, Celina's anger died. Why blame him? If it hadn't been Danny it would have been something else dragging Maressa into focus, and Celina had known it was only a matter of time before Maressa herself made a move. Danny's unthinking behaviour might have brought it forward a week or two, a month or two, but that was all.

'It's all right, Danny,' she reassured him. 'It's over and done with. Forget it. It doesn't matter.'

Danny brightened at once. 'Well, if you're sure?' he asked, mouth beginning to curve into its habitual smile. 'I've already had one roasting this morning so I was hoping you wouldn't be too hard on me.'

'Luke?'

'Uh-huh.' Danny nodded. 'He was volcanic, almost blasted me to hell and back. Funny thing,' he told her confidentially. 'I've lived with Luke for nearly twenty-seven years and never realised he had such a temper. Still, that's love for you. When you finally fall, you fall good and hard.'

Celina merely nodded, allowing Danny to wander off, relieved and happy at having made his peace. She didn't bother pointing out the flaws in his reasoning. He'd work those out for himself if the penny ever dropped that men caught cheating on their wives behaved in exactly the same way Luke had—they went on the defensive. And Danny had overlooked something else as well, something glaringly obvious to Celina: Luke *had* been in Paris that weekend. And so had Maressa.

'Telephone, Celina. I think it's the nursing home.'

'Thanks, Anita.' Celina hurried into the office, a chill of premonition running through her. She picked up the phone, listening to the short message in silence, the colour draining from her face, knuckles standing out white and stark as she gripped the mouthpiece.

'I'll be there as soon as I can,' she said, replacing the receiver and standing perfectly still, rooted to the spot, staring blindly at the notice-board in front of her. A rustle of clothing behind her made her turn her head.

'Bad news?' asked Anita gently.

'Yes! No! I—that is, they're not sure,' she stammered, seeing Anita through a sudden blur of tears. 'Something's happened. They've taken him to hos-

pital—for surgery. If it all goes right it could be what
I've hoped for, prayed for. But if it goes the other
way—— Oh, God!' She crumpled. 'I'll never get there
in time. What if I'm too late?'

'You sit there.' Anita took control. 'I'll phone for a
taxi and while you're waiting I'll make you a hot drink.
No arguments,' she added as Celina made to protest.
'Five minutes spent composing yourself won't make
much difference, will they?'

Celina sat down. Anita returned with a cup of hot,
sweet tea and by the time she'd finished it the first impact
of shock had begun to wear off.

She dried her eyes and climbed into the taxi. She sat
ramrod-straight, hardly noticing the streets through
which they travelled, nothing registering on her mind
apart from the urgent need to reach the hospital as
quickly as possible. It was the crisis point, in more ways
than one, and Celina had a feeling deep in her bones
that nothing would ever be the same again.

It was the longest three hours of her life, sitting alone
in a waiting-room, drinking the cup after cup of hot tea
that arrived from heaven only knew where, but she went
home at the end of it having sat with her father for a
precious five minutes, a tiny seed of hope growing in
her heart. He was alive, he'd come through the operation, and, though it would be another few days before
the doctors could say for certain, they were quietly op-
timistic that Celina would soon be taking him home.
And that, of course, meant telling Luke.

She asked to be put down a few blocks from their
apartment. She would walk the last mile; she needed the
fresh air. She'd wondered fleetingly how Luke was going
to react but she'd shied away from the picture that had
sprung to mind. This was the end. It had to be. Without
Maressa they might have stood a chance. Luke would
have been annoyed at Celina's deception but he would
have understood; she was beginning to see that now,

wishing she'd been honest from the start. And yet why blame Maressa? The marriage was doomed. For Luke it was just another business deal, a 'fixed-term contract...with an early-termination clause'. Oh, yes, she remembered the wording. It was carved in giant letters on her heart.

She didn't have long to wait. Luke came straight across, pulling her into his arms. 'I know, Celina, I know,' he told her, voice full of some strange, indecipherable quality that for a fleeting moment Celina took for empathy.

Her composure crumbled, the events of the day suddenly all too much for her. 'You've been sp-spying on me,' she accused absurdly, burying her head deep in his chest.

Luke's hands stroked her hair, long, sweeping, soothing movements. 'No, my love, you don't understand. Let me explain,' he said, the merest hint of a smile in his voice. 'Let me explain.'

Celina snapped then, resenting his amusement, taut nerves stretched to breaking-point, a welter of emotions battling for supremacy. The anger won, anger bottled up and corked but now bursting out, unstoppable. Anger at her father's wasted years, anger at a God who could sit back and watch it happen, anger at this man holding her close, who could marry without love, who could play games with her life, could mouth empty platitudes.

She sprang out of his grasp, pushing him away, eyes wild, hair flying about her shoulders. 'Don't touch me,' she spat, backing away from him. 'I don't want your excuses, I don't want your understanding, I don't want your money, and most of all, Luke, I don't want you.'

'Celina, love, you don't know what you're saying,' he appealed, spreading his arms.

'And don't "Celina, love" me either in that mealy-mouthed tone you wouldn't use to a four-year-old. I don't want to know how you found out—I can hazard a guess,' she told him bitterly. 'You've gone too far this time with your sleazy investigations. The game's over, Luke; finished. I've had enough. Go back to Maressa. It's what you've wanted all along in any case.'

'No, Celina, you're wrong, you're not thinking straight. I know you're upset but if I could just——'

'Go to hell,' she interrupted, twisting away as he tried to approach her. 'I want nothing from you; nothing at all. Why, I wouldn't even thank you for the time of day.'

He took a step nearer. 'You're not being fair, Celina. You've had a shock, you're overwrought, but if you'll just sit down and listen for a moment——'

'No!' she spat. 'I'm through listening to you. You've lied to me, you've been lying all along, tricking me into this empty shell of a marriage, arranging my life for me, organising Danny's for him. You're power-mad, do you know that, playing games with people's lives and emotions? Well, here's one life you're no longer going to control. We're through, Luke. Not that we ever got started, not really.'

'What are you doing?' he asked as she dashed across the room and into their bedroom.

Celina flung open the wardrobes, dragging down the cases, tossing them on to the bed. 'What does it look as if I'm doing?' she asked witheringly, opening drawers and removing clothes at random. 'Packing for my holidays? I'm leaving, Luke. Going. Departing. Walking out. Quitting. Decamping. How many more verbs does it take to get the message across?'

'Listen to me, Celina. For heaven's sake, listen to me.'

She ignored him. She filled once case, slammed it shut, locked it, started on another.

Luke came up behind her, spinning her round, gripping her shoulders with fingers that bit cruelly into her flesh. 'Listen, you little fool,' he hissed, shaking her. 'You don't know what you're doing, and you don't know what you're saying, and in the circumstances I refuse to meekly stand and watch while you walk out like this.'

'Just try stopping me,' she warned, voice rapier-sharp. 'You no longer own me, Luke Sinclair. Our contract is terminated, as of now. I'm a free woman. I'm leaving, and there's not a single thing you can say or do to stop me. There's nothing left, you see?' she found herself explaining with deliberate cruelty, needing to hit out, wanting to hurt. 'Nothing left at all. There's nothing I need. *You've* nothing I need. In short, Luke, you're now surplus to requirements. And could you please remove your hands?' she ended venomously. 'You're hurting me.'

He released her at once. Celina returned to her packing. She was acutely aware of him standing at her side, watching, waiting, and then he sighed heavily. With slow, deliberate movements he crossed to the door.

'I'll pour you a brandy. I think you need it. Don't argue, Celina. Another five minutes won't make much difference, will they?'

That was the second time today she'd heard those words. Celina straightened, looking at him properly for the first time. He was pale, pinched, and she felt her heart turn over. She did still love him, after all. If only—— But no! He didn't love her. That had changed. And she couldn't live with him day in and day out, wanting his love, knowing she could never have it, listening for his step in the hall, his voice of greeting, his easy smile, and all the time waiting for the day when he walked in and demanded his freedom. It was more than she could bear. Life without him might be hell. Life with him, on those terms, was unendurable.

Luke was watching her, his expression bleak. She hardened her heart. 'Five minutes,' she mocked cruelly. 'You were once worth ten, I seem to remember. How the mighty do fall.'

He flinched visibly, but he didn't reply, just stood there, very still, until Celina began to rummage in the wardrobe, and then he went out, quietly, closing the door behind him.

Hearing the click, Celina felt the sting of tears and stopped what she was doing for a moment, allowing them to run unchecked down her cheeks.

'I'll move out,' he told her ten minutes later. 'No arguments, Celina. You've nowhere to go. Use a bit of sense. I can move in with Danny. I'll just pack a few things and then I'll be out of your way.'

He waited for an answer but Celina didn't give one. She'd accepted the brandy with a slight inclination of the head, and now she sat and cradled the glass, not particularly wanting it but taking occasional sips to give herself something to do.

Luke shrugged and went to pack.

'I'll be off, then.' His voice cut into her thoughts.

Celina looked up briefly, her eyes darting away as they made contact with his. She nodded.

There was an awkward pause and Celina sat rigid, guessing he had something else to say and wishing he'd just go, leave her alone, leave her with her misery.

'You will get in touch if there's anything you need, won't you, Celina,' he said at length, adding very softly, 'Anything at all?'

Celina laughed, a mirthless sound, filling her ears, echoing horribly inside her head. 'If I were burning in hell, Luke, and you were my only hope of salvation, I'd still choose to take my chances with the devil. That's how much I need anything from you.'

The parcels arrived the following morning, Celina's heart turning over as she registered automatically the foreign stamps and the Paris postmark. She thought at first they were for Luke and was putting them on the table when her own name leapt out at her.

Intrigued, she cut away the string on the smaller one, the outside wrappers falling away to reveal the distinctive Laroche logo.

Celina gasped, the awful truth hitting her at once. That's how Luke had bumped into Maressa, innocently and completely unplanned. No wonder he'd been angry, refusing to explain. Celina had reached the obvious conclusion, allowing Maressa's cleverly planted insinuations to fester in her mind. And, if she was wrong about that, what else could she be wrong about?

She'd cried herself dry in the night, tossing and turning on the tear-soaked pillow, closing her eyes, trying to block out the memories, the happy times, the light-hearted moments. She kept telling herself that it was all an illusion, a pretence, simply part of a game invented by Luke, but it was little consolation. It didn't take away the pain, nothing would.

And now? The pain deepened. She lifted the exquisite gown from its nest of tissue-paper, tears coursing silently down her cheeks. She'd hurt him. She hadn't trusted him at all. Luke wasn't playing games with Maressa, he'd no need to. He was much too strong a character to need another woman as a shield. Luke had been honest from the start about his reasons but Celina hadn't believed him. She'd formed her own ideas and, like a fool, she'd clung to them, jealousy colouring her view. And she couldn't even apologise. All those angry words and poisoned gibes had poured out unchecked and they could never be unsaid.

If only she could turn back the clock. Just twenty-four hours—that would be enough. It didn't matter how Luke had found out about her father. Celina had thought it did, and maybe that was true at first, but not any more. And now it was too late. Whatever chance they'd had, Celina had killed it. She'd live with that knowledge for the rest of her life and it seemed such a terrible price to have to pay.

*   *   *

The low buzz of the lift pierced her fragile consciousness. Celina turned in surprise, her cheeks flaming as Luke stood framed in the doorway.

'I got your note,' he said awkwardly. 'Thank you.'

'No. Thank *you*. The dresses were beautiful, and I'm sorry, Luke; I jumped to the wrong conclusion.'

'Hardly surprising in the circumstances. I guess I should have explained there and then, but——' he paused, and shrugged eloquently '—but I didn't, did I?'

'No.' She held his gaze for an instant and then dropped her eyes, walking with wooden steps across to the window. She was wondering why he'd come. It couldn't just have been the note. It had been brief and simple and hadn't needed a reply.

'Can I sit down?' he asked.

Celina's eyes widened. He almost sounded nervous. 'It's your flat,' she pointed out tonelessly.

'No, it isn't. You live here. I'm a visitor, unless you want it otherwise.'

'I'm not staying,' she said, ignoring his comment. 'I'll be out of your way very soon, and then you can move back in.'

'No. I can stay with Danny. You don't have to pack up and leave in a hurry, Celina. You don't even have to go. Take as much time as you need before you make a decision.'

'I want to go,' she told him simply. 'I've somewhere in mind for Dad and me.'

'Ah, yes, of course. Your father's on the mend, so Roger tells me. You must be very relieved.'

'Roger?' Celina queried, startled.

'We were at school together,' Luke explained. 'We were best friends. I pop across to see him whenever I can.'

'I see.' Celina turned back to the window as another piece of the jigsaw slotted into place. Another coincidence, another irony, and another of her glaring mistakes. She wondered fleetingly how close she'd come to bumping into Luke on her Thursday-afternoon visits to the nursing home, and as the picture flashed into her mind the ghost of a smile crossed her lips.

'I came to apologise,' Luke said, breaking into her thoughts. 'I misjudged you. I was wrong all along. I'm sorry.'

'For what?' Celina asked, spinning round. 'I'm the one who was in the wrong, Luke, not you. I was the one jumping to all the wrong conclusions, refusing to allow you to explain. You've done nothing to reproach yourself with. If that's why you've come you could have saved yourself a journey.'

'I wanted to come.' His voice rose. 'You're a stubborn woman, Celina. Won't you let me explain once and for all? You've never really listened to me, have you?' he demanded with unexpected vehemence.

'I'm sorry,' she said simply, taking the chair opposite.

'And stop telling me you're sorry,' he rasped, eyes flashing daggers across at her.

Celina's eyebrows rose in surprise but she bit back an angry retort, waiting patiently for Luke to speak. When he did it was a low and completely toneless explanation.

'I stopped you marrying Danny because I thought you were taking him for a ride, taking his money. It was only later that I found out you hadn't touched a penny.'

'Not entirely,' Celina admitted, her heart sinking as she forced herself to level with him. There'd been too many half-truths already; this time she was keeping nothing back. 'In fact, I did take money from Danny.'

'Oh, Celina, Celina,' he laughed, a flash of humour crossing his face, lightening his features for an instant. 'A few thousand pounds. A loan which you did your damnedest to repay. I know about that. But that's peanuts in comparison. Danny was down tens of thousands and, like a fool, I blamed you.'

'I *was* the obvious culprit,' Celina pointed out, doing her best to lessen some of his guilt. It was an easy mistake to make and yet he was punishing himself.

'Too obvious,' he rasped bitterly. 'Why didn't you tell me I was wrong, Celina? You must have realised that everything I said, all those cheap and nasty comments, were unjustified, and yet you said nothing. Why?'

'Were they?' she asked, raising quizzical eyebrows. 'Think about it. Every single thing you mentioned applied to me. Everything. The money. My reasons for wanting to get married. The other man. All true. And if they were true they must have been justified. In any case, I couldn't take the risk. You wanted someone with no ties, no family commitments. How could I tell you that I'd lied and expect you to honour our arrangement? You'd thrown me a lifeline; I couldn't risk your cutting it. Besides,' she lifted her chin defiantly, troubled eyes meeting his, holding his, 'I valued your good opinion and was so afraid you'd hate me, resent me for tricking you, despise both me and my father.'

Luke flinched visibly. 'What do you take me for?' he asked in anguish. 'I would have understood. I'm flesh and blood and I do have feelings. I might have been angry at first but that's all, believe me, that's all. And when I did find out the truth...' He paused and shrugged again, his features darkening. 'If I'd been honest with you, Celina, we might have avoided this whole tangled mess.'

'"If ifs and ands,"' she murmured, tears welling up, swamping her.

'Sorry?' Luke queried, leaning forwards, blond waves falling over his eye in sharp reminder of the way it did when they were making love.

'Nothing,' she replied, his face a sudden blur. 'Nothing important. It doesn't matter any more, does it, Luke? Nothing does.' It was over. He didn't despise her but he didn't love her either. And Maressa had won, as Celina had always expected. Clever, clever, Maressa. It hadn't been much of a fight, had it, in the end? One casually dropped remark, a single grain of poison, but Celina had swallowed the bait. She'd destroyed her only chance of happiness and she couldn't even blame the upset with her father. The whole day had been a nightmare, and yet when Luke had come forward to offer his support and understanding she'd tossed it all back in his face, lashing out, rejecting him. And now she'd lost him. The knife plunged deeper, the blade twisting and turning with deliberate brutality, slicing away at her soul. Oh, yes, it was definitely over.

'Thank you for coming,' she said brusquely, much sharper than she realised in her battle to keep back the tears. 'I'm glad we've cleared the air if nothing else. I'll be leaving on Monday,' she explained, jumping up, moving round the room, deliberately avoiding the pain in his eyes. 'I'll leave you my address and then anything I've left can be sent over. Goodbye, Luke,' she ended simply, imploringly, willing him to leave, the threads of self-control already starting to disintegrate. If he didn't go soon she would embarrass them both, and she couldn't bear that on top of everything else she'd put them through.

Luke sighed heavily. 'I told Danny it was a waste of time,' he murmured, standing up, picking up his raincoat. 'Why should I expect you to love me? You married me for love, all right, love of your father. Now he's getting better and I'm no longer needed. Still, it was a good try. Goodbye, Celina. I'll see myself out.'

An eternity passed. Celina stood very still, not believing what she'd heard. '*What* did you say?' she asked, holding her breath, her heart beginning to go thump, thump, thump in her breast.

'I said I'd see myself out.'

'No! Not that!' She gestured impatiently, the words in her head refusing to reach her lips.

Luke paused, an eyebrow raised in puzzlement.

'What did you say before you said that?' she snapped, her voice rising shrilly. 'Something about Danny. For goodness' sake, Luke, tell me what you said.'

'Danny seemed to have it fixed in his mind that you loved me. It was a stupid idea. I shouldn't have let him raise my hopes. Sorry, Celina. You can laugh if you want to.'

There was another charged silence while his words sank in. Celina continued to stare at him, stunned, the anguish of his face unendurable, while something deep inside began to glow, began to spread, began to fill her with a strange excitement. She might be wrong, very wrong, but she had to take the risk, and, if Luke laughed about it later with Maressa, well, she'd never know, would she? But she *had* to make sure for her own peace of mind.

She swallowed hard. 'Luke.'

'Celina?'

'I love you, Luke.'

'You love me?'

She nodded, stepping forward, eyes brimming over but a hesitant smile beginning to play about the corners of her mouth.

'You love me? You're sure?' he asked, the realisation dawning on his face, transforming his features.

'I'm sure. I love you, Luke. I've loved you from the start and I'll always love you.'

'Can I tell you something?' He moved quickly, the raincoat dropped unnoticed on the floor as he reached for her shoulders, eyes searching her face, the shadows of doubt disappearing as he read the truth reflected in Celina's shining eyes.

'If you must,' she teased, offering her mouth in silent invitation, savouring the touch of his lips on hers, the strength of his arms as they pulled her close.

'I love you, Celina. I love you. I love you. I love you. I've always loved you. I guess that's why I married you.'

'Are you sure?' she teased again, tilting back her head, her eyes full of love and fun as their glances locked and the message flowed out and across, one to the other and back again.

'Woman,' Luke growled, picking her up and striding forcibly across to their bedroom, 'you'd better believe it . . .'

'Hungry?' he asked a lifetime later, his lips still nuzzling her mouth. 'I meant for food,' he explained with a ripple of amusement as he caught the expression in her eyes. He planted a kiss on the tip of her nose. 'Won't be a moment. You stay right there.'

He padded out, naked, leaving her to curl up contentedly on the pillows, listening to the silence, picking out the sounds she'd never thought to hear again, the sounds of Luke in the apartment, in her life, and her mouth curved into a happy, satisfied smile.

She was still smiling when he returned with a tray, which he placed on the bed before climbing in beside her. He poured the wine, helping Celina to cheese and biscuits and pieces of fruit.

'You look like the cat that got the cream,' he observed with a grin.

Celina nodded. 'I feel like the cat that got the cream,' she agreed. And then something struck her. 'Luke?' she mused, studying his profile.

'Yes, my love?'

'Why wouldn't you make love to me after that first time? Why did you freeze me out?'

'Oh, that!' He turned to face her, suddenly serious, solemn blue eyes locking with hers. He leaned forward, cupping her face in his hands. 'I'd taken something very precious,' he told her. 'Something irreplaceable, something I didn't think I was entitled to, and hell, Celina, you've no idea how bad that made me feel.'

She kissed away the frown lines, slipping her hands round his neck, locking her fingers. 'And I thought it was Maressa.'

'Maressa?' He laughed. 'Oh, no, my love. Maressa was over and done with a long time ago.'

'But I didn't know that,' she pointed out, darts of pleasure running through her every time he said the magic words. My love. How natural it sounded. How wonderful it sounded!

'No. My fault. I just expected you to know. You *do* know now, though, don't you?' he asked anxiously.

Celina smiled happily. 'Yes, Luke.' She picked up her glass, which was filled to the brim and spilled over slightly, Celina giggling as the cold liquid splashed her. 'To us,' she toasted. 'With special thanks to Danny for bringing us together—twice!'

Luke grinned. 'And we won't be risking third time lucky either,' he told her emphatically.

'Have you really loved me all this time?' she asked, suddenly shy under the naked hunger of his gaze.

'From the moment you first walked in with Danny all those months ago,' he insisted. 'And I never for a moment stopped.'

'Not even when you thought the worst of me?'

'Not even then.' He hugged her fiercely. 'Not even then, I promise you. I must have known, mustn't I, deep down? And when I think of all those revolting accusations...' He paused, a shadow crossing his face, and Celina reached out, running a hand across his cheek, laughing as Luke caught her wrist, kissing her open palm. 'It doesn't matter now, does it?' he asked softly, fingers curling around hers.

Celina nodded. 'No, Luke. It doesn't matter at all.'

He drained his glass before taking Celina's from her, setting them down on the bedside table, and then he turned, eyes dancing merrily. 'And now, Mrs Sinclair,'

he bent and licked a tiny drop of wine which had slid
down her breast and was hovering in delicious invitation
on the tip of a nipple, 'guess what we're having for
dessert . . .'

4 FREE

Romances
and 2 FREE gifts
just for you!

*You can enjoy all the
heartwarming emotion of true love for FREE!
Discover the heartbreak and the happiness, the emotion
and the tenderness of the modern relationships in
Mills & Boon Romances.*

*We'll send you 4 captivating Romances as a special offer
from Mills & Boon Reader Service, along with the chance to
have 6 Romances delivered to your door each month.*

Claim your FREE books and gifts overleaf...

An irresistible offer from Mills & Boon

Here's a personal invitation from Mills & Boon Reader Service, to become a regular reader of Romances. To welcome you, we'd like you to have 4 books, a CUDDLY TEDDY and a special MYSTERY GIFT absolutely FREE.

Then you could look forward each month to receiving 6 brand new Romances, delivered to your door, postage and packing free! Plus our free newsletter featuring author news, competitions, special offers and much more.

This invitation comes with no strings attached. You may cancel or suspend your subscription at any time, and still keep your free books and gifts.

It's so easy. Send no money now. Simply fill in the coupon below and post it to -
Reader Service, FREEPOST, PO Box 236, Croydon, Surrey CR9 9EL.

NO STAMP REQUIRED

Free Books Coupon

Yes! Please rush me my 4 free Romances and 2 free gifts! Please also reserve me a Reader Service subscription. If I decide to subscribe I can look forward to receiving 6 brand new Romances each month for just £9.60, postage and packing free. If I choose not to subscribe I shall write to you within 10 days - I can keep the books and gifts whatever I decide. I may cancel or suspend my subscription at any time. I am over 18 years of age.

Name Mrs/Miss/Ms/Mr _____ EP18R

Address _____

_____

Postcode _____ Signature _____

Offer expires 31st May 1992. The right is reserved to refuse an application and change the terms of this offer. Readers overseas and in Eire please send for details. Southern Africa write to Book Services International Ltd, P.O. Box 41654, Craighall, Transvaal 2024.
You may be mailed with offers from other reputable companies as a result of this application.
If you would prefer not to share in this opportunity, please tick box. ☐

Mills & Boon

Forthcoming Titles

BEST SELLER ROMANCE
Available in February

DARKNESS INTO LIGHT Carole Mortimer
BLIND DATE Emma Darcy

COLLECTION
Available in February

The Betty Neels Collection
AT THE END OF THE DAY
NEVER THE TIME AND THE PLACE

The Patricia Wilson Collection
A MOMENT OF ANGER
BRIDE OF DIAZ

MEDICAL ROMANCE
Available in February

CAUGHT IN THE CROSSFIRE Sara Burton
PRACTICE MAKES PERFECT Caroline Anderson
WINGS OF HEALING Marion Lennox
YESTERDAY'S MEMORY Patricia Robertson

Next month's Romances

Each month, you can choose from a world of variety in romance with Mills & Boon. These are the new titles to look out for next month.

SUMMER STORMS Emma Goldrick

PAST PASSION Penny Jordan

FORBIDDEN FRUIT Charlotte Lamb

BAD NEIGHBOURS Jessica Steele

AN UNUSUAL AFFAIR Lindsay Armstrong

WILD STREAK Kay Thorpe

WIFE FOR A NIGHT Angela Devine

WEEKEND WIFE Sue Peters

DEAR MISS JONES Catherine Spencer

CLOAK OF DARKNESS Sara Wood

A MATCH FOR MEREDITH Jenny Arden

WINTER CHALLENGE Rachel Elliot

CASTLE OF DESIRE Sally Heywood

CERTAIN OF NOTHING Rosemary Carter

TO TRUST MY LOVE Sandra Field

STARSIGN

SHADOW ON THE SEA Helena Dawson

Available from Boots, Martins, John Menzies, W.H. Smith, most supermarkets and other paperback stockists.

Also available from Mills and Boon Reader Service, P.O. Box 236, Thornton Road, Croydon, Surrey CR9 3RU.